BABA DUNJA'S
LAST LOVE

Alina Bronsky

BABA DUNJA'S LAST LOVE

Translated from the German
by Tim Mohr

Europa
editions

Europa Editions
214 West 29th Street
New York, N.Y. 10001
www.europaeditions.com
info@europaeditions.com

Translation by Tim Mohr
Original title: *Baba Dunjas letzte Liebe*
Translation copyright © 2016 by Europa Editions

Library of Congress Cataloging in Publication Data is available
ISBN 978-1-60945-333-6

Bronsky, Alina
Baba Dunja's Last Love

Book design and cover illustration by Emanuele Ragnisco
www.mekkanografici.com

Prepress by Grafica Punto Print – Rome

Printed in the USA

BABA DUNJA'S
LAST LOVE

I'm awoken in the night again by Marja's rooster, Konstantin. He's like an ersatz husband for Marja. She raised him, and she pampered and spoiled him even as a chick; now he's full-grown and good for nothing. Struts around the yard imperiously and leers at me. His internal clock is messed up, always has been, though I don't think it has anything to do with the radiation. You can't blame the radiation for every stupid thing in the world.

I lift up the covers and let my feet drop to the ground. On the floorboards is a carpet I crocheted out of strips of old bedsheets. I have a lot of time in winter because I don't have to tend to my garden. I rarely go out during winter, only to fetch water or wood or to shovel snow from my doorstep. But it's summer now, and I'm on my feet at five in the morning to go wring the neck of Marja's rooster.

Every morning I'm surprised when I look at my feet, which look knobby and swollen in my German hiking sandals. The sandals are tough. They'll outlive everything, surely including me.

I didn't always have such swollen feet. They used to be delicate and slim, caked with dried mud, beautiful without any shoes at all. Jegor loved my feet. He forbade me to walk around barefoot because so much as a glance at my toes made men hot under the collar.

When he stops by now, I point to the bulges protruding from the hiking sandals and say, See what's left of all their splendor?

And he laughs and says they're still pretty. He's been very polite since he died, the liar.

I need a few minutes to get my blood pumping. I stand there and brace myself on the end of the bed. Things are still a bit hazy in my head. Marja's rooster Konstantin is screeching as if it's being strangled. Maybe someone has beaten me to it.

I grab my bathrobe from the chair. It used to be brightly colored, red flowers on a black background. You can't see the flowers anymore. But it's clean, which is important to me. Irina promised to send me a new one. I slip it on and tie the belt. I shake out the down-filled duvet, lay it on the bed and pat it smooth, then put the embroidered bedspread on top of it. Then I head for the door. The first few steps after waking up are always slow.

The sky hangs light blue over the village like a washed-out sheet. There's a bit of sunlight. I just can't get it through my head that the same sun shines for everyone: for the queen of England, for the black president of America, for Irina in Germany, for Marja's rooster Konstantin. And for me, Baba Dunja, who until thirty years ago set broken bones in splints and delivered other people's babies, and who has today decided to become a murderer. Konstantin is a stupid creature, always making such a racket for no reason. And besides, I haven't had chicken soup in a long time.

The rooster is sitting on the fence looking at me. Out of

the corner of my eye I see Jegor, who's leaning against the trunk of my apple tree. I'm sure his mouth is contorted in a derisive sneer. The fence is crooked and leaning precariously, and it wobbles in the wind. The dumb bird balances atop it like a drunken tightrope walker.

"Come here, my dear," I say. "Come, I'll quiet you down."

I stretch out my hand. The rooster flaps his wings and screeches. His wattle is more gray than red, and it shakes nervously. I try to remember how old the creature is. Marja won't forgive me, I think. My outstretched hand hangs in the air.

And then, before I've even touched him, the rooster falls at my feet.

Marja said it would break her heart. So I have to do it.

She sits with me in the yard and sniffles into a checkered handkerchief. She has turned her back to me so she doesn't have to see me plucking out the pale speckled feathers and tossing them into a plastic bag. Down floats on the air.

"He loved me," she says. "He looked at me a certain way whenever I entered the yard."

The plastic bag is half full. Konstantin is nearly indecent, naked in my lap. One of his eyes is half-open, gazing up at the sky.

"Look," she says. "It's like he's still listening."

"There's certainly nothing he hasn't heard out of you before."

That's the truth. Marja always talked to him. Which makes me worry that I'll have less peace and quiet now. Aside from me, everyone seems to need somebody to talk to, and Marja more than most. I'm her nearest neighbor, the fence is all that divides our properties. The fence might have been solid at some point. But these days it's not much more than a notion of a fence.

"Tell me exactly how it happened." Marja's voice is like a widow's.

"I told you a thousand times already. I came out because he was screeching, and then he suddenly fell over. Right at my feet."

"Maybe someone put a curse on him."

I nod. Marja believes in that stuff. Tears run down her face and disappear in the deep wrinkles of her face. Even though she's at least ten years younger than I am. She doesn't have much of an education, she worked as a milk-maid, she's a simple woman. Here she doesn't even have a cow, though she does have a goat that lives with her in the house and watches TV with her whenever there's anything on. At least that way she has the company of a living, breathing entity. Except the goat can't hold up its end of the conversation. So I answer.

"Who would want to put a curse on your stupid bird?"

"Shhh. Don't speak ill of the dead. Anyway, people are evil."

"People are lazy," I say. "Do you want to boil him?"

She waves her hand dismissively.

"Fine. Then I'll do it."

She nods and looks furtively at the bag of feathers. "I wanted to bury him."

"You should have told me earlier. Now you'll have to

bury the feathers with him so his people don't laugh at him in heaven."

Marja thinks for a moment. "Ach, what's the point. You cook him and give me half of the soup."

I knew it would work out that way. We don't eat meat very often, and Marja is a glutton.

I nod and pull the shriveled eyelid down over the rooster's glassy eye.

The stuff about heaven I didn't really mean. I don't believe in it. I mean, I believe there's a heaven above our heads, but I know that our dead aren't there. Even as a little girl I didn't believe that people snuggled in the clouds like in a down-filled duvet. But I did think you could eat the clouds like cotton candy.

Our dead are among us, often they don't even know they're dead and that their bodies are rotting in the ground.

Tschernowo isn't big, but we have our own cemetery because the people in Malyschi don't want our corpses. At the moment their city council is debating whether to require a lead coffin for Tschernowo corpses buried there, because radioactive materials continue to give off radiation even if they're no longer alive. In the meantime we have a provisional cemetery here, in a spot where a hundred and fifty years ago a church stood and thirty years ago a village schoolhouse. It's a humble plot with wooden crosses, and the few graves there aren't even fenced in.

As far as I'm concerned, I don't even want to be buried

in Malyschi. After the reactor mishap, I left like almost everyone else. It was 1986, and at first we didn't know what had happened. Then liquidators showed up in Tschernowo in protective suits, carrying beeping devices up and down the main street. Panic broke out, families with little children were the fastest to pack up their things, rolling up mattresses and stuffing jewelry and socks into teakettles, roping furniture to their roof racks and roaring off. Speed was now a necessity, since it wasn't as if the mishap had taken place the day before, it was just that nobody had told us about it until then.

I was still very young, fiftysomething, but my children were no longer at home. So I wasn't too worried. Irina was studying in Moskow, and Alexej was on a tour of the Altai mountains. I was one of the last to leave Tschernowo. I helped others to stuff their clothes in sacks and to rip up floorboards to get at the money they'd hidden underneath. I didn't really see why I should leave at all.

Jegor shoved me into one of the last cars that was sent from the capital and squeezed in beside me. Jegor had let himself get swept up in the panic, as if his balls needed to produce any more children and needed to be rushed to safety. Despite the fact that he'd long since drunk his crotch sterile and limp. The news of the reactor brought him temporarily to his senses, and he started yammering on about the end of the world and got on my nerves.

I don't have any large pots at home because I've lived alone since I returned. Houseguests aren't exactly lined up around the block. I never cook to save leftovers, I always cook fresh every day. Borscht is the only thing I warm up day after day. But it gets better with every day it sits.

I take the biggest pot I can find out of the cabinet. And look for a top that will fit. I've accumulated a lot of tops over the years, none of which fit properly, but they're good enough for me. I cut the head and feet off the rooster, they'll go into the soup. Then I cut off the rump, which I give to the cat. I put the rooster in the pot along with the head and feet, a peeled carrot from the garden, and an onion with the skin on so the broth will have a nice golden color. I pour water in from the bucket, just enough so everything is covered. It'll be a nourishing broth, fatty and glistening.

When the reactor happened, I counted myself among those who got off lightly. My children were safe, my husband wasn't going to live much longer anyway, and my flesh was already toughened with age. In essence I had nothing to lose. And anyway, I was prepared to die. My work had taught me always to keep that possibility in mind so as never to be caught by surprise.

I marvel every single day at the fact that I'm still here. And every second day I ask myself whether I might be one of the many dead who wander around unwilling to acknowledge that their name is already inscribed on a gravestone somewhere. They need to be told, but who is that brazen? I'm happy that nobody has anything left to say to me. I've seen everything and have no more fears. Death can come, just let it come gracefully, please.

The water in the pot is bubbling. I turn down the heat, grab a ladle from a hook, and begin to scoop off the thick gray foam that's pushing up the sides of the pot. If the water were to keep boiling so hard, the foam would break up into tiny bits and get mixed into the broth. On the ladle the foam looks dreary and unappetizing, like a collapsed gray cloud. I let it drip into the cat's bowl. Cats are even less sensitive than we are. This cat is the daughter of the one that was in my house when I came back. She was really the lady of the house and I was just her guest.

The nearby villages are all abandoned. The buildings are still there, but the walls are flimsy and collapsing, and the nettles grow as high as the eaves. There aren't even rats because rats need garbage, fresh, greasy garbage. Rats need people.

I could have taken my pick of houses in Tschernowo when I came back. I chose my old one. The door was open, the gas tank was only half empty, the well was just a few minutes' walk away, and the garden was still recognizable. I cleared the nettles and cut back the blackberries, for weeks I didn't do anything else. I knew: I need this garden. I can't manage the walk to the bus stop and the long ride into Malyschi very often. But I need to eat three times a day.

Ever since, I've planted a third of the garden. That's enough. If I had a large family I would use the entire garden. I benefit from the fact that I took such good care of it before the reactor. The greenhouse is a jewel, handcrafted by Jegor, and I harvest tomatoes and cucumbers a week before everyone else in the village, just as I did before the reactor. There are gooseberries in green and red and currants in red, white, and black, old bushes that I carefully prune each fall so they produce new shoots. I have two apple trees and a raspberry patch. It's a fertile area here.

The soup is simmering on the lowest flame. I'll let it cook for two or even better three hours, so the old flesh softens and falls from the bone. It's the same with people: it's hard to choke down old flesh.

The smell of the chicken soup makes the cat twitchy. She slinks around my feet, meowing, and rubs herself against my calves in their thick wool stockings. I know I'm getting older because I'm always cold. Even in summer I don't leave the house without wool socks.

The cat is pregnant, I'll give her the skin and gristle of the rooster later. Sometimes she hunts beetles and spiders. We have a lot of spiders in Tschernowo. The amount of bugs has increased since the reactor. A year ago a biologist came and photographed all the spiderwebs in my house. I leave them be, even when Marja calls me a slovenly housewife.

The good thing about being old is that you don't need to ask anyone's permission anymore—you don't need to ask whether you can live in your old house, or whether it's okay to leave the spiderwebs be. The spiders were here before me, too. The biologist took pictures of them with a camera that looked like a weapon. He set up spotlights and lit up every corner of my house. I didn't have any objection, no reason he shouldn't go ahead and do his job. He just had to turn down the sound on his device because the beeps sent chills down my spine.

The biologist explained to me why we have so many bugs. It's because there are far fewer birds in the area since the reactor. So the beetles and spiders can multiply unhindered. He was unable to tell me, however, why there are so many cats. Cats probably have something that protects them against bad things.

A second cat slips into the doorway. The cat that lives with me immediately arches her back. She's a beast and doesn't let anyone across the threshold.

"Come on, be nice," I say, but she isn't nice. She makes hissing noises and her hair stands on end. She has only half a tail, someone clipped off the rest. I always had cats and chickens and, earlier, a dog, it's a part of village life that I like. Another reason I came back. The animals here aren't sick in their heads the way they are in the city, even if they are irradiated and crippled. The noise and constriction of the city makes cats and dogs crazy.

Irina flew all the way from Germany just to try to keep me from moving back to Tschernowo. She tried all means, even crying. My Irina, who never cried, not even as a little girl. It wasn't that I forbade her to cry; on the contrary, it would have been healthy to cry sometimes. But she was like a boy, climbing trees and fences and sometimes falling off, even getting smacked, and still she never cried. She ended up studying medicine and now she's a surgeon with the German military. That's my girl. And then, of all times, she thought she needed to cry because I wanted to move back home.

"I have never told you what you have to do," I explained to her. "And I don't want you to tell me what I have to do."

"But, Mother, who in their right mind could possibly want to go back to the death zone?"

"You're saying words that you don't understand, my girl. I've already gone to look, the buildings are all still standing, and weeds are growing in the garden."

"Mother, you know what radioactivity is. Everything is irradiated."

"I'm old, nothing can irradiate me anymore, and even if it does it's not the end of the world."

She dabbed her eyes dry in a way that made it clear she was a surgeon.

"I won't come visit you there."

"I know," I said, "but you don't come very often anyway."

"Is that a reproach?"

"No. I think it's good. Why should anyone hover around their parents?"

She had looked at me suspiciously, like she used to many years before, when she was still little. She didn't believe me. But I meant it just as I said it. There's nothing for her here, and I don't try to make her feel guilty about that, either.

"We can meet every couple of years in Malyschi," I said. "Or whenever you come. As long as I live."

I knew she didn't have a lot of vacation days. And when she took them she didn't need to spend them here. And back then flights were still really expensive, far more expensive than they are now.

There was one thing we didn't talk about. When something is particularly important, you don't talk about it. Irina has a daughter, and I have a granddaughter, who goes by the very pretty name of Laura. No girls are named Laura around here, only my granddaughter who I have never seen. When I went back to the village, Laura had just turned one. When I went back home, I knew I would never see her.

Grandchildren always used to leave the cities during their summer breaks and stay out in the country with their grandparents. The school holidays were long, three hot summer months, and the parents in the cities didn't have such long vacations. It was the same in our village, from June until August city kids ran around and in no time at all they had sunburned faces, bleached hair, and dirt-crusted feet. They went together into the woods to pick berries, and they swam in the river. Noisy as a flock of birds they went up and down the main road, stealing apples and wrestling in the muck.

When they got too wild, we sent them out into the fields to collect potato bugs, which threatened our crops. They would pick them off the plants by the bucket-load and then burn them. I can still hear the sound of all the shells popping in the fire. We really miss the little thieves now—the world's never seen a plague of potato bugs like the one we've had since the reactor.

Everyone in Tschernowo knew that I was a nurse's assistant. I was always called when children had broken something or had abdominal pain that wouldn't stop. Once a boy had eaten too many unripe plums. The fibers caused a blockage in his gut. He was pale and writhing around on the floor, and I told them to get him to the hospital immediately, and the boy was saved by an emergency operation. There was one with appendicitis and another who turned out to be allergic to a bee sting.

I liked the children, with their fidgety feet, scratched-up arms, and high-pitched voices. If there's anything I miss these days it's them. Those of us who live in Tschernowo these days don't have any grandchildren. Or if we do we never see them. Except maybe in a photo. My walls are covered with pictures of Laura. Irina sends me new ones in almost every letter.

It probably wouldn't take Laura long to become a care-free summer holiday child. If everything were like before. Though it's hard for me to imagine it. In her baby pictures she had a serious little face, and I wondered what sort of thoughts lived in her head to project such darkness from her eyes. She never wore bows or barrettes in her hair. Even as a baby she didn't smile.

In the most recent photos she has long legs and hair that's almost white. She still looks very serious. She's never written to me. Her father is German. Irina promised me a wedding photo—one of the few promises she hasn't kept. She always sends greetings from him. I collect all the letters from Germany in a box in my dresser.

I never ask Irina whether Laura is healthy. I never ask about Irina's own health, either. If there's one thing I'm afraid of, it's the answer to that question. So I just pray for them, even though I don't believe there's anyone who listens to my prayers.

Irina always asks about my health. When we see each other—every two years—the first thing she always asks about is my blood counts. As if I have any idea. She asks about my blood pressure and whether I've had a breast cancer scan.

"My dear girl," I say, "look at me. Do you see how old I am? And I made it this far without vitamins or operations or checkups. If something bad manages to worm its way into me now, I will leave it be. I don't want anybody touching me or sticking needles in me, and that much I have earned."

Irina shakes her head. She knows that I'm right but she can't escape her surgeon's mind-set. At her age I thought the same way. And the way I was at her age, I would have picked a huge fight with the me of today.

When I look at our village, I don't feel as if it's nothing but a collection of living corpses running around. Some people won't last long, it's true, but the reactor alone isn't to blame for that. There's not many of us, you can count us all on two hands. Five or seven years ago there were more of us, when all at one time a dozen people followed my example and moved back to Tschernowo. We've buried a few of them in the meantime. Others are like the spiders, resilient even if their webs are a bit erratic.

Marja for instance is a little crazy with her goat and her rooster, which is simmering so nicely in my pot. Unlike me, Marja knows her blood pressure exactly because she takes it three times a day. If it's too high she gulps down a pill. If it's too low she gulps down a different pill. That way she always has something to do. But she's bored anyway.

She has a medicine cabinet that could kill the entire village. She restocks it regularly in Malyschi. She takes antibiotics for a cold or diarrhea. I tell her she shouldn't take them, that they actually do more damage than good, but she doesn't listen. I'm too healthy, she says, I wouldn't understand. And it's true, I can't remember the last time I had a cold.

The aroma of the chicken broth fills my whole house and wafts out the window. I pull the rooster out of the pot and lay it on a plate to cool. The cat brays and I raise a cautionary finger at her. I fish out the vegetables, too, they've already lent the broth their flavor and now they're just limp. I wrap them in an old newspaper and take the bundle out to the compost pile. There are pumpkins growing on my compost pile, in the fall I'll harvest them and pass them out to people in the village, otherwise I'll have to eat gruel with pumpkin all winter.

I pour the broth through a sieve into a second pot. A thousand fatty golden eyes peer up at me from the new pot. I read in a newspaper that you should skim off the fat. But I disagree. If you want to live, you have to eat fat. You have to eat sugar once in a while, too, and first and foremost lots of fresh fruits and vegetables. In summer I eat cucumber and tomato salad almost every day. And herbs by the bunch, they grow thick and green in my garden— dill, chives, parsley, basil, rosemary.

The meat isn't too hot anymore, I can touch it with my fingers. I carefully remove it from the bones and put it in a bowl. I used to cut it up into small pieces for my children and make sure I divided it evenly between them. Even though Alexej was just eighteen months younger than Irina, he was a skinny little fellow, and I was sometimes tempted to save the best bits for him.

We ate a lot of chicken soup because there were a lot of chickens in Tschernowo. I made borscht and *schi* and *solyanka* from the broth. It was never boring. I can picture Irina cutting meat into small bites for Laura when she was younger. If Laura was here, I would tell her what her mother was like as a child. But Laura is far away and stares out at me from the wall with sad gray eyes.

The day goes by quickly when you have things to do. I tidy up the house. I wash a few pairs of underpants and hang them on the line in the garden. The sun dries and bleaches them, and it takes just two hours before I can fold them and put them away.

I scrub the dirtied stockpot with sand, rinse it with well water, and leave it, too, to dry in the sun. I have to take a break at some point, and I sit down on the bench in front of the house with a newspaper. I get the papers from Marja. She found them in her house when she moved in. The single woman who used to live there had read a lot of papers, including the good women's papers: *Factory Woman* and *Woman Farmer*, every issue. Bundles of them, each bound with twine, were stacked under the bed and in the toolshed. Marja gave them all to me. I read them whenever I have time during the day and also before I fall asleep at night.

In the issue of *Woman Farmer* I open are recipes using sorrel, a sewing pattern, a short love story set on a collective farm, and a disquisition on the theme *Why women shouldn't wear pants in their free time.* It's from February 1986.

I pour half of the soup into a smaller pot and look around for a top that will fit it. Holding it by the handles, I carry it over to Marja's. I have to suddenly blink as I pass the fence because Konstantin's ghost is sitting there swaying in the wind. I nod at him and he answers by flapping his wings wildly.

Cats are crowded in front of Marja's house, and no wonder: it smells like valerian inside. Marja is a large woman, particularly in width. She's sitting in armchair and her body arches over the backrest. Her gaze is fixed on the TV, which is equipped with two antennas. The screen is black.

"What's on today?" I ask and put the pot on the kitchen table.

"Nothing but shit," says Marja. "Same as always."

That's why I never turn on my television. I dust it off once in a while and the cat likes to sleep on top of it, on a doily. On my last visit to Malyschi I saw in a shopwindow that there are now TVs you can hang on the wall like a painting. Marja's by contrast is like a potbellied chest, and it takes up half the room.

"What did you bring?" She doesn't turn toward me because it's difficult when you're wedged into a chair the way she is.

"The soup," I say. "Your share."

She immediately starts to cry and the goat, which is lying in Marja's bed, adds a baleful "meeeeeh."

When I get out a bowl, I can't help but notice that Marja has really let things get out of hand lately.

Her dishes are covered with a fatty film, which tells me she's scrimping on soap. The sink is stopped up and moldy. And this woman says I should clear out the spiderwebs in my place. There's a pile of colorful pills on the table.

"Marja," I say sternly, "tell me, what's going on?"

She waves my question off with one hand and with the other rummages around between her breasts. From between various layers of unwashed clothing, she pulls out a photo and hands it to me.

I push my glasses up to my forehead and hold the picture closer to my face. It's a black-and-white photo of a couple: a girl in a white wedding dress with a long train, and a fellow with broad shoulders and a low forehead in a black suit. The girl is heartbreakingly beautiful: big eyes beneath thick lashes and a mouth that promises sweet kisses. She looks fragile in the slightly too big dress that's not been fitted quite right. And although the contrast couldn't be more stark, I recognize immediately that the girl is Marja.

"That's your Alexander?" I ask.

And Marja cries more and says that she got married fifty-one years ago today.

I should have realized that Marja isn't just lazy and messy. She's lazy and messy because she's suffering from depression. Back when I was a nurse's assistant nobody had depression and when people killed themselves you called them insane, unless it was out of love. Later on I read in a newspaper that there was such a thing as depression, and I asked Irina about it on her last visit.

She looked at me as if she didn't want to answer at first. She wanted to know why I was asking, like it was some kind of state secret.

I told her I just wanted to know if there was anything to it. And Irina said in Germany it's very widespread, practically like a stomach bug.

And when I look at Marja, I think maybe it sloshed across the border at some stage. Perhaps if she'd moved back to Tschernowo earlier, she could have avoided it—if there's one thing that can't harm us here, it was the epidemics that sweep through the rest of the world.

Marja has told me a lot about her Alexander. Most importantly, that he beat the living daylights out of her and at some point while in a drunken stupor got run over by a tractor. She took care of him for a while after that, and he continued to curse her and to throw his cane—and whatever other heavy objects he could grab—at her from bed. A few days before the reactor he threw a radio at her and managed to hit her. The radio was totally destroyed, which made Marja so upset that she left with the liquidators and a sack of clothes without ever turning around to look at Alexander. He was discovered only after he was dead, and now she's reproaching herself and painting a rosy picture of her past.

I'm of only one mind about that sort of thing: when two adults live together but have no children, they can just as well live apart. That's not a marriage, that's just a lark.

But I keep my opinion to myself.

I thoroughly wash two of Marja's bowls and dry them with a dish towel that turns out to be a piece of curtain. Marja mutters to herself that I'm wasting her water and that she's too weak to go to the well. I click my tongue, she needs to pipe down.

She wrenches herself out of the armchair and comes to the table. Her body is massive and the rickety dining chair groans beneath her backside. It's a mystery how someone can get so fat in a village where you have to either grow all your food or drag it all laboriously home from town.

I shove a bowl of chicken soup over to her.

As she takes the spoon in her hand, dunks it in the golden broth, and guides it to her lips, I suddenly see it: Marja as a young bride with a fear of the future flickering in her eyes. Her former beauty hasn't completely disappeared, it's still here in the room like a ghost. How much easier I've had it my entire life: never being beautiful means never being afraid of losing your beauty. Only my feet drove men wild, and now I can't even cut my toenails. Lately Marja has helped me do it.

The goat jumps out of Marja's bed and comes over to us at the table. It puts its head on Marja's lap and peers over at me. I take a mouthful of soup, which is clear and salty like tears.

And I think to myself that Marja should never have come here. It's not the radiation. It's the peace and quiet that is so bad for her. Marja belongs in the city, where she can quarrel with the baker every morning. Since nobody here has any desire to fight with her, she's lost her sense of self and just sits around stewing, and she's wilting as a result.

There are about thirty houses lining our main road. Not even half of them are inhabited. Everyone knows everyone else, everyone knows where the others are from, and I suspect everyone could tell you what time of day his or her neighbors go to the bathroom and how often they turn over in their sleep. Which doesn't mean that everyone here spends time together. People who move back to Tschernowo have no desire for companionship.

Money is also a factor. There are places available in Malyschi, but the gray five-story buildings from the Khrushchev era have leaky pipes and thin, moldy walls. Instead of gardens there are courtyards with a rusty swing, the remains of an old slide, and a row of never-emptied garbage barrels. Anyone who wants to plant tomatoes needs a dacha outside of town, to which an overly crowded bus goes once a day. I would have to have rented, and my pension would have only been enough to cover living with strangers as a lodger. And the room would have been tiny.

Though we do have people in Tschernowo for whom money is not an issue, as far as I can tell. The Gavrilows, for instance, are educated people, I can tell from the tips of their noses. And also by the fact that they are accustomed to living in comfort. They could win prizes for their garden. They have a raised bed with cucumbers, a greenhouse, and a contraption that they grill meats on during the warm months, just like on television. And they have roses, a never-ending supply of roses in every color, which grow in bushes that entwine the fence. Mr. Gavrilow often stands in front of those roses in a suit, and as soon as he catches sight of a withered blossom he cuts it off. Mrs. Gavrilow dabs the leaves with a soapy cloth to ward off aphids. When you walk past their property it smells like honey and perfume. But they never speak to anyone, so if I urgently needed salt I'd go somewhere else.

I could go to Lenotschka, who from the back looks like a girl and from the front like a doll. A doll like the ones Irina had, but aged for decades. Lenotschka mostly sits in her house, knits an endlessly long scarf, and smiles when someone addresses her. Doesn't answer, though. She has a lot of chickens, and they seem to multiply at her place like flies. I could go to Lenotschka if I needed something, she always shares if she has it.

I would go to Petrow, too, except that he has no salt in his home. He is cancer-ridden from head to foot. After his operation they wanted to keep him in the hospital to die. He fled like he was in prison, jumped out the window in his surgical gown, his IV pulled along behind him. He moved into the house of his ex-wife's grandparents in Tschernowo and didn't have much more in mind than to die quickly and peacefully. But that was a while ago now. He's been here for a year, to date the last one to arrive. Petrow doesn't grow anything in his garden because he says he doesn't want to feed the cancer anymore. He considers salt and sugar unhealthy, so he doesn't have either in his home.

I put in a spoon, carry the bowl of chicken soup across the street, the German hiking sandals raise dust. I call loudly at Petrow's gate, and when he doesn't answer I walk in. He is still alive, and he emerges from the hedges zipping up his fly. A hatchet with a rusty blade is stuck in his belt. Beneath his left arm he squeezes a yellowed little book that he probably found in some empty house. The first few months he annoyed the whole of Tschernowo knocking on doors and asking for reading material—he had arrived with nothing but a bag with underwear and a notebook in it.

"Greetings, Baba Dunja," he says. "I'm not much when it comes to gardening, and these blackberries are wearing me out." He shows me his scratched arms and I shake my head apologetically.

"What's new in *Woman Farmer*?" he asks.

His skin is so translucent that I wonder if perhaps he has become a ghost after all.

"You need to eat something," I say. "Otherwise you won't have any strength."

He sniffs the bowl.

"Your fat friend's old rooster?"

He sure shoots his mouth off for someone so translucent.

"That's why it's finally quiet," he says, sniffing the soup again.

"Eat."

"That stuff will kill you. Salt, fat, animal protein."

I'm a peaceful person, but I'm slowly developing an urge to dump the soup down his front.

He seats himself on the bench in front of the house and polishes my spoon with his shirt.

"I like you, Baba Dunja," he says. The spoon shakes in his hand. He probably hasn't eaten in days.

"Come over whenever you are hungry," I say. "I always cook fresh."

"I may be an asshole but I'm no freeloader."

"You can thank me by repairing my shutters."

"Look what I found," he says conspiratorially, reaching behind his back.

I have to push my glasses up to the top of my head in order to make it out. A pale blue packet of Belomor cigarettes, dented, with the letters on the label running together.

"Where did you get that?"

"Found it behind the couch."

"Looks empty."

"There are three left."

He holds the packet out to me. I pull out a bent stalk. He pulls out another and clamps it between his teeth. Then he gives me a light. The smoke burns in my throat.

"You're no freeloader," I say. "You are a generous man, you share your last cigarette with me."

"I'm already regretting it." He sucks on his greedily, the same way he just spooned up the soup. "I'm no gentleman."

My cigarette goes out with a fizzle. Either I did something wrong or it is old and damp. Petrow pulls it out of my mouth and lays it carefully on the bench next to him.

"Now I have a bellyache," he says. "My stomach is full of dead old rooster. That soup will be the death of me."

I pluck a large leaf from the fat thistle that is trying to pry

Petrow's house out of the ground with its roots and wipe the bowl with the leaf. I can't remember the last time I smoked.

My sight has deteriorated but I still hear perfectly. Which certainly also has something to do with the fact that there's little noise in the village. The whir of the electrical transformer hums in my ears as steadily as the buzz of bumblebees or the song of the cicadas. Even here the summer is a rather loud time. In winter it's stiller than still. When there's a blanket of snow on everything, even your dreams are muted, and only the bullfinches hopping through the undergrowth provide any color in the white landscape.

I don't worry about what could happen if one day we no longer have electricity. I have my kerosene cartridges, and there are candles and matches in every house. We are tolerated, but none of us believes that the government would come to our aid if we used up all the resources. That's why we think in terms of self-sufficiency. Petrow has taken to using the neighboring house to heat his own during the winter. There's enough wood.

The biologist told me that not only do the spiders weave different webs here, the cicadas also make a different sound. I could have told him that, anyone with ears can hear it. The biologist doesn't know why, though. He recorded their songs with his machines and listened to them with a notepad and a stopwatch. He took more than a dozen cicadas to his university in a see-through box with holes in it. He promised to let me know if he figured it out. I've never heard from him.

We are not easily reached in Tschernowo. Actually completely unreachable, particularly if one doesn't wish to be reached. We have postboxes in Malyschi. Whenever someone goes there, he or she brings a bundle of mail for the others. Or not.

I never ask anyone to bring me anything because I always have mail in my box and it's heavy. Irina sends me packages. Alexej does not. I'm not sure which one of them I'm more grateful to.

If I were to stack up all the packages that Irina has sent me from Germany, the pile would be several stories high. But I fold up the yellow cardboard containers neatly and carry them to the shed. Everything that Irina puts in the packages seems very carefully thought out. Smoked sausages and preserves, vitamin pills and aspirin, matches, thick socks, underwear, hand soap. A new pair of glasses, prescription sunglasses, toothbrushes, pens, glue. A thermometer, a device to measure blood pressure (which I gave to Marja), and batteries of all kinds. I have a collection of brand-new scissors, pocketknives, and little digital alarm clocks.

I look forward to the German gelling sugar, which isn't available here, because it means I don't have to simmer my jams for hours. Same goes for the baking powder and the spices with Latin letters on them, the little baggies of bean and tomato seeds (though I like to cultivate my own). I give away the large boxes of adhesive bandages and the rolls of gauze bandaging.

I used to often write to Irina that I don't lack for anything. Or almost anything. She could send me seeds from her region so I could get to know something new. But she doesn't need to feed me from Germany. Then I realized that she needs the packages more than I do. Ever since, I just say thank you and every once in a while mention things I might want. Like for example gummi bears and a new potato peeler.

What I await anxiously are the letters. A letter is always a party. I don't even need to buy a newspaper, but I buy one anyway when I go to Malyschi, just to see a bit of what's going on in the world. I read the newest letter every night before I go to bed, until the next one arrives.

Petrow says that these days nobody writes letters anymore and that messages are sent from computer to computer and telephone to telephone. And some even from computer to telephone. In Tschernowo there are no telephones, that is, the devices themselves are here but there aren't any functioning lines. A few people have little handheld phones but they only have reception when you get closer to the city. Petrow has one, he showed it to me. He plays stacking games on it like a little kid.

When he was new in town he trudged around town holding his phone up. "No reception, no reception," he yammered and suggested we collect signatures to petition for a transmitter tower. Nothing came of it.

The Gavrilows said that anyone who wanted to make phone calls didn't belong in Tschernowo. Marja said the things gave off radiation. Old Sidorow, who is at least a hundred years old because he was already old when I was still young, Sidorow said his landline functioned perfectly and that Petrow could use it anytime he wanted, the way it should be among neighbors.

He showed us his old phone, it consisted of a plastic housing that must have been orange at some point, with a handset and rotary dial. It was sitting on Sidorow's table between some gigantic yellow squashes he had just harvested.

Petrow picked up the handset and held it to his ear. Then he passed it around.

"Kaput," said Marja, handing the phone on to me. I hung up.

"The line is dead, Opa," said Petrow. "All the lines here are dead, do you understand? All of them."

Sidorow insisted that he regularly—not every week, but almost—spoke to his girlfriend in the city.

"Natascha," Sidorow clarified, seeing my skeptical look, then he pointed to Marja. "A little younger than her."

Later Petrow tried to convince me that old Sidorow wasn't all there. I just shrugged my shoulders. If there was one person who shouldn't have been casting stones, it was Petrow.

I sit on the bench in front of my house as Sidorow shuffles by, propped up with a cane. He doesn't look too well, either. After a few steps he turns around and walks wearily back. He straightens himself up in front of me, everything on him is trembling. If he had more teeth they would be chattering.

Then he asks me why I don't invite him in.

So I invite him in. Except for the spiderwebs, my sitting room is clean and tidy, and guests can stop in anytime. I'm prepared. Although I hadn't expected Sidorow. He lowers himself onto a chair, places his cane between his knees and his hands on the tabletop. I set the teakettle to boil.

He's wearing an old gray suit that is worn but clean. His legs are bony and his beard is scraggly and wiry.

"Dunja," he says. "I'm serious."

"What are you serious about?" I ask.

"I'm about to tell you."

I give him time. The kettle whistles, I put broken peppermint sprigs into two teacups and pour hot water over them. I let my cup sit so it will cool off a little. Sidorow sips his tea immediately and asks for sugar.

I get a packet out of the cabinet. It's old and the cubes of sugar are crumbly. I don't put any in my tea because pure sugar makes one anxious and greedy.

Sidorow drops two cubes into his cup and tries to stir it. The sprigs of mint get in his way.

"I want to tell you something," he warns me.

"I'm all ears."

"You are a woman."

"True."

"And I am a man."

"If you say so."

"Let's get married, Dunja."

I choke on the mint tea and cough until my eyes start to water. Sidorow watches my coughing fit with sympathy. As I pull out my handkerchief to wipe my face, he seems to attribute the tears to my emotions.

He clears his throat. "Don't get the wrong idea. I like you."

"I like you, too," I answer automatically. "But—"

"So it's settled," he says, standing up and getting ready to leave.

I'm speechless for a moment. Then I collect myself and catch him at the door. "Where are you off to so quickly?"

"To get my things."

"But I didn't say yes."

He turns and looks at me, his eyes pale blue like the summer sky above the village. "What did you say then?"

I guide him back to the chair and put the teacup in his hand.

"I don't want to get married, Sidorow. Not to anyone. Never again." On the back of my hand, there where the thumb meets the hand, is a small faded tattoo that I did myself with a needle and ink when I was fifteen. And now, of all moments, it starts to itch. These days it looks more like a flyspeck than a letter of the alphabet.

"Why not?" A childlike wonder shines in his eyes.

"I didn't come here to get married."

He sniffs huffily. Then he stands up again with an effort. "Think it over. I could repair your fence."

"Why now?"

"Because we're not getting any younger."

"I thought you had a girlfriend in the city?"

He sniffs again and waves his hand dismissively. His departure cannot be hindered any longer. I take him to the door and watch as he walks down the street and the cane raises little clouds of dust. A puff of wind makes the back of his shirt billow.

I've known him my whole life. Other than me, Sidorow is the only one who lived in Tschernowo before the reactor. When I was still a little girl he was a grown man with a family, and a head taller than I was. I lost track of him after the reactor. When I moved back to Tschernowo he apparently read about me in the newspaper. In any event he was the next to come, and I never asked him what had become of his boisterous wife and their two sons.

I can pretty well imagine what put thoughts of marriage in his head. He is a man and when his things become caked with dirt he washes them with household soap in a wash pan only to hang them to dry in the garden without rinsing them. For food he wets a bowl of oats twice a day with watered-down milk if he has it and with springwater when the milk is gone. On holidays he adds frosted corn flakes or colorful fruity loops from a big box with a foreign logo on it. His vegetables spoil because he has a green thumb but can't cook.

Me on the other hand, I cook fresh every day and my garden thrives.

I haven't been to Malyschi in more than a month. If it was up to me I wouldn't be in any rush to go back. But my provisions are depleted, the butter and oil, the semolina and the alphabet noodles. The evening before, I get my rolling basket out of the shed and clean off the spiderwebs. The spiders work quickly, we should follow their example. It makes me think of the biologist and the fact that he had collected the webs so cautiously, with tweezers, and deposited them in a canister.

I can't see anything special about the webs. They're silvery and sticky.

I ask Marja if she needs anything from the city, I ask Petrow, and think about asking Sidorow, too, but then I leave it be. I don't ask the Gavrilows. Lenotschka doesn't answer when I knock. Marja asks for magazines, knitting wool, and a bunch of pills, including some for constipation. I'm not going to bring knitting wool. There are piles of holey wool sweaters in her wardrobe that she can unravel. My basket will be full enough as it is.

Petrow asks me for good news.

"Don't joke around," I say. "I can bring you honey."

"I don't want any honey," he says. "I don't eat honey because it's made of bee vomit. Bring me good news."

That's how he always is.

In the morning I get up before five. The ghost of Marja's rooster is sitting on the fence looking at me reproachfully, but at least he's quiet. I wave to him and start to get ready for the trip to the city. Since I got the hiking sandals I no longer have to put lotion on my feet before a long march, that's how comfortable the shoes are. I put on a fresh blouse and an old skirt that feels a bit loose, apparently I've lost weight. I get money out from under the dirty laundry pile in the cabinet and put it in my wallet, and the wallet I stick in my brassiere.

I don't need to write a shopping list, I have it all in my head. I slice a fresh cucumber and put the slices in a plastic container that Irina sent me last year filled with paper clips. I have no idea what I would do with paper clips, but the container is useful. I don't salt the cucumber because I don't want it to lose too much water in transit. There are still a few pieces of the homemade bread I left in the sun to dry into zwieback, and I take those, too. The food you get in the city doesn't agree with me.

It's a long trek, and I know that by evening the fresh socks in my hiking sandals will be dusty. A year ago it still only took me an hour and a half to make it to the bus stop, but now it takes over two. A few years ago I still used to ride my bicycle but now I feel too unsteady. The Gavrilows always go by bicycle but they never ask if they can bring anything. It's probably to do with the fact that they are the only couple and can't imagine what it is like alone.

I can't help thinking of Jegor and our wedding. It was a huge wedding, the whole village celebrated. I had a small wedding ring and he had none at all because we wanted to save for the child that was growing in my belly. At thirty-one I was an old bride. Originally I hadn't planned to say yes to Jegor. Three long years we used to meet up before the child nestled inside me and surprised us both. I had thought myself barren. And even though I knew that older first-time mothers experienced more problems and had sick children, the pregnancy was like a miracle to me.

After we'd been to the civil registry office and everyone had eaten and drunk, I took off my shoes in the yard and danced. All the men sang, whistled, and howled. Jegor pulled me out of the middle of them, pushed me into a corner, and said that from now on I had to keep my shoes on. He gestured like he was going to step on my bare toes with his heavy boots. I knew I had made a mistake.

I don't hold it against Jegor; most men were like that back then. The mistake wasn't picking the wrong one. The mistake was marrying at all. I could have raised Irina and Alexej myself, and nobody would have been able to stipulate what I did with my feet.

The bus stop is called "Former Golden Rabbit Factory" and it's the last stop on the 147 line to Malyschi. The old factory is a few hundred yards from the stop. It's an abandoned brick building with looming towers. The windows are all broken. Inside you can see rusty machines in an eternal state of sleep.

I can still remember how, earlier, so many people from Tschernowo and neighboring villages used to ride to the factory by bus or bicycle to work on the conveyor belt. The pralines were very good, dark, melting chocolate shells, a filling with little pieces of nuts, packed in gossamer paper and then wrapped in foil and another sheet of paper that had a picture of a little rabbit and her baby rabbits on it. For the New Year's holidays, the foremen received a special collection in a giant gift box. Just thinking about the fillings made my mouth water back then: jelly, cognac, truffle cream.

For special occasions I bought a handful of pralines for Irina and Alexej, and once a patient who supervised the night shift at the factory gave me one of the New Year's gift boxes. He had probably received two. It was great fortune.

We opened the box, as was intended, when the clock struck midnight. We divided each praline into three—Jegor didn't eat any. The box lasted for three-quarters of a year. We kept the packaging, too: out of the foil we made ornaments for the New Year's tree the following year, and the rabbit paper we flattened between the pages of books and hoarded like treasure. The children traded pieces of the rabbit paper for other praline wrappers with bears and foxes and red-cheeked, pigtailed girls on them.

When my children were little there were none of the overpoweringly scented stickers that come in packs of Turkish chewing gum that I smelled for the first time in the nineties, before I moved back to Tschernowo. In Tschernowo there was no Turkish gum, no counterfeit Chanel perfume or fake cognac, no girls with lurid make-up on their faces, no faded jeans, and no shrill music. In

Tschernowo there was just silence and me. A few months later Sidorow arrived, and then the lights came on in one house after another.

The memory makes my mouth fill with sticky saliva. I had once been a sweet tooth, but these days the thought of chocolate just makes me feel sick. I'd rather eat currants from my garden than cream-filled pralines. It's a function of age and my pancreas. I pull a small bottle with a twist cap out of my bag and drink a sip of springwater.

I sit on the bench, the factory at my back, and look out at the dry, summery yellow landscape. The fields haven't been tilled for decades but they have retained their structure. Here and there scattered ears of grain grow skyward, grain that reseeds itself year after year. If you walked on you could find corn, sugar beets, and potatoes. They've been grown over by thick, green weeds, by large-leafed plants with light purple stems the name of which I don't know because it wasn't around during my youth.

The bus station shelter is painted green and clean. Nobody would come this far to scrawl on it. The area is considered scary. The factory is in what many call the death zone. Tschernowo is deeper inside the zone. This bus station marks the border. A soldier with a machine gun used to stand here, bored to death. These days the border is no longer guarded. In the Ukraine, on the other hand, they make a big drama over their zone, with barbed wire and guard posts. Petrow told me that. I understand less and less of what happens beyond the border.

All of us in Tschernowo know the bus won't keep running for much longer. What we'll do then, we don't know. Maybe by then there will be someone who can bring us the things from Malyschi that we can't grow ourselves. Petrow already tried to hire somebody, but nobody would do it. We scare people. They seem to believe that the death zone stops at the borders people draw on maps.

It's a joy every time the bus turns up.

I had to wait for less than an hour and could enjoy the fresh air in peace and quiet and lose myself in my thoughts. The few kilometers from the village to the bus stop are no longer just a stroll at my age. When I return, my basket will be full and the walk will feel even longer.

The driver has been driving this route for five years. His name is Boris and a year and a half ago his first grandson was born. I cautiously ask how the baby is doing. It's a delicate subject and I don't want to cause anyone pain. Boris answers hoarsely that the boy has a good appetite and is growing well.

I exhale.

He takes the exact change from my hand. The transit authority hasn't raised the fare for thirty years. You couldn't even get a glass of water for this amount in Malyschi anymore. It's fine by me, my pension hasn't gone up at all either.

I sit in the front so I can chat with Boris. He has a big belly and slumped shoulders, and there's something in his face that makes me nervous. When I was a nurse's assistant I was often called to men like him who were lying next to a conveyor belt or in a garage with cardiac arrest.

We have more than an hour's ride together. The road is bumpy, gravel shoots out from under the tires as they labor along the unpaved surface. The little bus shakes and the soccer team pendant hanging from Boris's mirror rocks back and forth.

I look out the window, hawks circle above the fields, between the trees I see a deer and a rabbit. The animals seem to act as if they discovered the area for themselves. We pass two abandoned villages on the way to the city, a cat sitting on the main street of one, licking its paw.

Boris tells me what he's seen on television. Lots of politics in the Ukraine, in Russia, and in America. I don't pay too close attention. Politics are important, of course, but at the end of the day, if you want to eat mashed potatoes it's up to you to put manure on the potato plants.

The important thing is that there's no war. But our president will see to that soon enough. Sometimes I feel queasy about the fact that Irina now has a German passport.

The jerking of the bus makes my old bones rattle, and I have the impression that one can hear them clanking against each other. I doze off now and then. When I open my eyes we are in the middle of the city. Boris steers his way through the rust buckets at the bus station to a parking spot at the rear.

The noise in Malyschi seems to get more deafening all the time. Despite the fact that there are fewer and fewer people on the streets, even here at the bus station there are at most a half dozen bus drivers and twenty passengers waiting in various lines. But they are all making a racket. I'm not used to it anymore.

My objectives are set. First I'll go to the bank where Irina opened an account for me into which my pension gets paid. Even though I can't buy anything at home, I withdraw it all because life has taught us not to trust the banks.

There are machines in the foyer of the bank. A girl with a scarf asks if I need help. I don't need help, I just need my money, and not from a machine but from a person at a counter. So I go into the main room. While I'm waiting, an icy wind blows up my calf and I'm happy about my wool stockings. When finally it's my turn, I mention the chilliness. The girl at the counter, who smells of perfume and chewing gum, says proudly that they have an air conditioner now. She looks as if she has never in her life had a potato bug on her hand. I see the goose bumps in her décolleté and warn her that she will catch a cold. She says she's had a cold for ages and shoves me the money from my pension, which I count and then divide into two halves and put into the cups of my bra.

Every time I pick up my pension I have an intense desire to buy something for Irina, Alexej, and Laura. When Laura was first born I sent her things, teething rings, rattles, leggings, until I realized that nobody needs that stuff. There are nicer things in Germany anyway. Maybe the tomatoes are bigger here, but the rompers are better there.

That's why I stopped buying useless things and instead put all my money in my old tea caddy. When Laura is eighteen, and that will be very soon, I will give it all to Irina, except for a reserve fund for my funeral. I will ask Irina to change the money into marks or dollars and put it into Laura's piggy bank. Laura is the youngest member of our family and young people need money.

Irina always corrects me, tells me that the mark no longer exists, but I can never remember what they have instead.

Next I go to the post office and on the way I pass the market. I indulge myself with a break, go into the market hall, which smells of fish and rotten vegetables, and lean against a stand selling crullers. The scents drifting by bother my nose. I eat a piece of cucumber from my garden.

The vendor looks down at me from the stand and I realize that it bothers him when I stand in front of his stand and eat something I've brought with me. It's impolite of me. I reach for my bag and apologize to him. He just throws his hand up and continues to stare at me. Then he asks me if I am Baba Dunja from the death zone.

I could ask him where it is he thinks he is right here. But I don't. If he feels safe here behind his greasy rings then let him indulge himself. Not to mention that I'm flabbergasted he knows me. I can't get used to it.

He hands me a baked good in oily paper. "On the house," he says. I don't want to offend him and take it even though I know that so much as a bite would ruin my pancreas.

"Do we know one another?" I ask and act as if I'm going to take a bite. When I was a nurse's assistant lots of people knew me, even in the neighboring villages. They always came to me when something was wrong. But in Malyschi they had their own doctors and nurses even back then. Maybe this man is from one of the villages. I have a good memory, but it contains only the faces of the children.

I ask him who he is.

He says I wouldn't know him but that everyone here knows me because they all talk about me. And the other returnees.

He turns and rummages in a box for a newspaper in order to show me something, but I tell him it's not necessary. I don't need to know what somebody said about me or, worse, wrote about me. In the past few years reporters have come again and again and taken photos of our gardens and asked us questions.

"I have to get going," I say and leave the market hall. The cruller I wrap more tightly in the paper and then in a napkin from my basket. Then I stow it in the basket. Marja will be pleased.

There's a big sign at the post office saying it's closed for lunch. I look at the clock. It's a bad sign if they are already on lunch break shortly before eleven, they're going to be a while. I go to the park, sit on a bench, and catch my breath. Walking on asphalt is poison for your joints, and the air is also polluted.

The park might as well be a cemetery, there's just one young couple hugging on the lawn. I sit with my back to them so as not to make them feel bashful, and fan air on myself with a magazine I've just bought for Marja at a kiosk. It's one of those foreign magazines that now has a Russian edition. The pages glisten, there are lots of pictures of thin women in sumptuous clothing. At the back are recipes, but they're mind-boggling to me. I don't know what tahini is and I've never even heard of risotto. I only know cream of rice with apples, maybe risotto is a foreign word for that.

Once I've rested sufficiently, I'm on my way again. I pass the time by going shopping. I buy cream that won't spoil in the heat, cheese, a ballpoint pen, and notepaper with roses on it. I want to write to Laura. I buy salt and five lemons. I see plastic containers with colorless mushrooms which are marked "imported champignons," the word "imported" is in block letters and underlined.

I buy three bananas and eat one straightaway. Bananas

are baubles for the senses, they're really too sweet but they are nice to chew on. I tuck the peel into my basket until I come across a garbage bin.

At the pharmacy I look at the list of medicines Marja has given me and grab this one or that one from the shelves. The ones I regard as nonsense I don't buy. Then my gaze falls on a pallet of pain relievers and I buy a huge container just to be safe.

My basket is filling up. I haven't gotten much for myself. That's good because it means more money is left over for Laura. I go back to the post office and see that the sign is gone.

Marja's postbox is empty. I won't tell her, I'll say they were being strict again today and wouldn't let me pick up her mail without authorization. There are three packages and five letters in my box. I stow everything well so nothing will get broken. It's late, the air smells smoky, and I need to get back to the bus station.

It's still light when I arrive in the village. The summer nights are long and merciless, there's a buzzing restlessness in the air, even here. Nobody is visible on the main street. The door to Sidorow's place is open. There is motion behind the windows at Marja's. She hasn't been sleeping well of late. That's why she gulps down colorful pills that make her wake up late and then leave her staring into space with glassy eyes.

Petrow is lying in his hammock with a book. The Gavrilows are sitting in front of their house playing chess.

I need to sit down. The city sucks the strength right out of you. After I've taken my shopping inside, I sit on the bench out front.

I take off my hiking sandals, which suddenly feel too small, and can hardly suppress a groan.

I strip off the wool stockings, my feet appear. If one were to add up all the time these feet spent dancing it would surely be more than a year. If I were to count the distance in dance steps it would be many kilometers. Now I have calluses and corns, and the nails are yellow and warped.

I place my feet in a bucket of ice-cold springwater. Beneath the surface of the water they look blurry. The cold creeps up my legs enlivening the old veins and withered muscles.

I take my feet out and put them on a terrycloth towel. I'd love to dry the toes individually but I can't reach them.

I go into the house barefoot, the wood floor is warm and mop-clean. I turn on the light in the kitchen and set the teakettle to boil. I eat the little piece of cheese that I bought in Malyschi with a cracker and a sprig of red currants. I can't figure out how I survived the years I spent in the city after the reactor without breaking down. Maybe it was the work that gave me strength. I knew that every pair of hands was needed in the public hospital and didn't allow myself to be forced into retirement. I was nearly seventy when I turned my back not only on the hospital but on the city, forever.

Before I go to bed, I open one of the letters. Opening mail from Irina isn't something I could ever do quickly or casually. I need to sit, I need to have time, my head needs to be clear. I don't want to be disturbed by a knock at the door. Now is actually an ideal time, and I grab the letter that was sent most recently. Something seems different. The envelope is white, and below the foreign postmark are my name and the address of the postbox, but not written with the surgeon's hand of Irina, which renders them uncomplicated like a man's writing. These letters are round and sweet.

I cut open the envelope with a knife. I already figured there wouldn't be any photos of Laura inside because the envelope is thin and feels soft. A sheet of paper falls out.

I shift closer to the lamp and push my glasses up on my head. My heart pounds. Normally I have a calm, level-headed heart. But whenever I begin to read a letter from Germany it races right up to the moment when it becomes clear that everyone is alive and healthy and that, at least in this particular letter, there's no bad news.

This time I have to make many attempts and still I don't understand a thing, and my heart continues to beat loudly. The letter is signed by Laura. But it's not in Russian. Without my previous job experience I wouldn't have been able to decipher the style of lettering. Some doctors write their diagnoses in Latin letters instead of Cyrillic.

I lie awake trying to calm my heart until dawn starts to break. The uneasiness just won't let up. I hear my own breathing, labored and wheezing.

I don't fear death. But in moments like these, when I have no peace of mind, I remember what it is like to be afraid. Not about the children, but about myself. It's stupid to cling to a body that has already been through it all. But these moments demonstrate to me that I'm not as ready as I might think. There are still things that need to be arranged. Words that need to be written. When I'm no longer around I don't want it to be any more burdensome than it has to be for Irina and Alexej.

In my head I begin to organize all that I absolutely need to take care of so I feel better prepared. It settles me down a bit. In fact, I give up on my plan to go ask Marja for some valerian oil. If Konstantin were still around he would be crowing now. But it's only his ghost sitting on the fence squinting at me reproachfully.

I put on a cardigan, shove Laura's letter into the sleeve, and from my rolling shopping basket take a packet of coffee from Irina's parcel and the bag of medicines for Marja. The letters from Irina I picked up the day before are all sitting open on the table. Contrary to my usual habit, I rashly read them all at dawn, one after the next. The usual—the weather, work, the European Union. No explanation, no hint at what Laura could have written to me.

I go past Konstantin carrying all the stuff. It's eight in the morning by now. Marja is in bed sitting awake but ill-humored, a mountain of pillows behind her and a down comforter across her knees. I look around for the goat. Maybe it's grazing out behind the house.

"Are you sick?" I unpack the things I've brought.

"As if you're healthy?" But Marja can't keep up her grumbling for long once she sees the new packet with foreign words on it. I'm just happy we have such bad reception here. If she could watch proper television she'd immediately need everything the pharmaceutical ads tout.

I wipe off a bronze coffeepot I find under some of

Marja's pots and pans. Then I count out the spoonfuls of coffee, pour in water from the canister, and stir thoroughly. I light the fire and let it heat up, holding the pot over the flames. Foam wells up, I skim it off and divide it into two cups. First comes the foam and then the strong, black coffee. My hand trembles as I pour it. It looks beautiful in the cup, the surface looks as if it is decorated with lace.

Marja sips her coffee and burns her mouth. She curses, the stuff is so bitter it could wake up the dead. It would be good enough for me if it just got her out of bed. She braided her blonde hair into two pigtails the evening before. During the night they've come apart, leaving the individual strands hanging. It occurs to me that Marja has hardly any gray hair.

"How was it in the city?" she asks.

"Same as always," I say. Although that's not true. Everything stands still here but the city changes constantly. Malyschi is dying. Other cities transform themselves in order to survive, but Malyschi can't manage it.

Laura's letter crackles in my sleeve. I had wanted to tell Marja about it, but I don't have the heart to. I keep Laura stashed so deeply inside me that I can't bring myself to talk about her. It would feel like exposing my innards.

"You're so strange today." Marja drops several sugar cubes into her coffee.

I get up from the chair, it's time for me to go.

"Hey, hey," she says, grabbing my skirt with her soft, white hand. "Stay a little while."

"Do you know German, Marja?"

"What would make you think that?"

Of course she doesn't. She probably wouldn't even recognize it if it were put in front of her.

"Could you tell the difference between German and English, Marja?"

"What on earth are you talking about?"

I sit down again. The feeling that I'm looking at the young woman from Marja's photo is so strong that I dry my eyes with a handkerchief so I can see her better.

"Fine. I'll stay a little longer."

Marja drinks down her sweetened coffee and drops her feet to the floor. They are bare, the toenails painted pink. They gleam like raspberry candies.

"You know," she says, "I'm so happy that you're back. Every time you go to Malyschi I worry that you will never come back."

There are days when the dead trip over one another on our main road. They talk all at once and don't even notice what nonsense they are speaking. The babble of voices hovers over their heads. Then there are days when they are all gone. Where they go, I do not know. Maybe I'll find out when I'm one of them.

I see Marina and Anja and Sergej and Wladi and Olya. The old liquidator in a striped shirt, his sleeves rolled up, with muscular forearms and polished shoes. He was a dandy at the outset. He died quickly.

The baby that was stillborn in my hands seven months after the reactor. I wrapped it up, unwashed, in a towel and handed it to the mother. She had given birth in her old farmhouse rather than in a birthing center. Se we had time and nobody disturbed us. The father turned away and left the room, the mother pulled open the corner of the towel and smiled. I knew what that smile meant. She would soon follow and thus didn't feel any sense of loss.

The little girl with red pigtails who didn't die so nicely, I'd have liked to give her something, but I wasn't permitted. The entire family badgered me and the doctor, demanding things that were out of our hands, fighting among themselves over trivialities.

Those are my dead, the ones that followed me to Tschnernowo, and there are dozens of others that were already here, along with their cats and dogs and goats. The village has a history that is intertwined with my history, like two strands of hair in the same braid. We've come part of the way together. I always greet the dead with a slight nod of the head, my lips barely move.

A man and a little girl are walking down the main road, I've never seen either one of them before. He's carrying a backpack, and she's pulling a small suitcase. Her feet are in red Sunday shoes. I greet them the same way I do the rest of the dead, but then I realize they aren't dead.

I stop and so do they. We look at each other. We never have visitors here, unless you count the film crews and photographers and biologists. And the nurse from the city who pops up every couple of years and wants to measure our blood pressure and take blood samples.

Her most recent visit was seven months ago, she was no longer wearing a radiation suit, just a lab coat, and too much rouge on her powdered, unnaturally white face. She parked her old Lada on the main road and tugged her equipment around behind her. Petrow closed the door in her face, Sidorow acted as if he couldn't see or hear her, Lenotschka smiled at her kindly and asked her not to touch her. Only the Gavrilows and Marja monopolize the poor woman's time and don't let her go until she has palpated their livers and tested their vision. When she knocked on my door, totally spent, I let her in and offered her a cup of tea. The harried look on her face and her bad perm reminded me too much of myself forty years ago.

People who come here normally stay until they are carried to a little plot by the former village school. The girl is probably terminally ill.

Even if I live to a hundred I will never learn to take something like that lightly. I look at the girl so intently that she nearly starts to cry. Then I introduce myself by name and ask what I can do for them.

The man doesn't want to say his name. He's different from all the others I've seen in these parts. He is a city person, but not from Malyschi. He's from the capital city. Everything about him, his shoes and his smooth face and his way of speaking, everything cries out that he doesn't belong here. I'm not the sort of person who quickly develops sympathy and he's making it particularly difficult for me to feel any towards him. The girl is named Aglaia. So it's true what Marja told me, that they name little girls like ancient women in the capital these days.

"Aglaia, right, so it's Glascha then," I say. The girl smiles and her hand moves from her father's to mine. She doesn't otherwise seem particularly trusting. Maybe I remind her of someone. She looks healthy, rosy cheeks, dark hair, only her eyes are sad, and her smile is crooked.

I lead little Glascha to a house that I want to show them. I nearly took it myself but it's too big for me. But the two of them need two rooms, it's not good when a girl and her father have to share a room. The eyes of the others follow us as we walk down to the end of the main road.

The house that I have in mind is painted blue. Glascha's eyes begin to light up and my heart softens. I force myself to let go of her hand. But she clings to me.

"Does it have running water?"

I don't look at her father as I answer. "Nobody here has running water. The well is at the end of the street. Some yards have their own, but not this one. We have electricity. There's a stove that you can heat and cook with. I don't know how long . . . "

I look at the girl and don't want to say it. It's not as easy in Tschernowo in winter as it is in summer. But will there still be two of them by then?

"I don't know, either," says the man.

He enters the gate. The girl lets go of my hand and follows him. She runs through the garden and I'm reminded of the fact that Irina and Alexej used to play here, too. An old woman, Baba Motja, lived in this house back then, and she let the village children munch her raspberries. She had not only red ones but also a yellow kind that Irina sometimes brought me, closed carefully in her fist so as not to squash the delicate berries. Yellow and larger than ordinary raspberries, they shone in the palm of her hand. But they didn't taste particularly sweet.

Glascha's father goes into the house and tries to open the window from inside. He has to tug and jiggle it, but then his face appears in the window, looking suddenly content. He disappears. There's a bustling sound and then something falls to the floor, and his upper body appears in the window again, as if he's framed in an old picture.

"Okay," says the man. "There's nothing better?"

If at my age I still spent time wondering about people I'd never manage to get around to so much as brushing my teeth.

"No," I say. "This is the best place as far as size, furnishings, and condition are concerned."

He seems surprised that I'm able to produce such long sentences.

"Okay," he says again. "Does it belong to anyone?"

"No," I say again. "You can live in it."

"And what if someone comes and demands I pay the rent retroactively?"

I don't begrudge him his suspicions. When it comes to the reactor, you can't trust anyone. There was a scandal just recently in our region. The residents of irradiated villages who moved to other places were promised compensation for their homes, and they claimed them at values the cabins wouldn't have had even if they'd been on Red Square. Bureaucrats dutifully approved them in exchange for a portion of the inflated compensation. At least that's how Marja told it. I was happy that on paper my house still belonged to me. Not to mention that my conscience is clear, which is something that becomes more and more important with age.

"Nobody just drops by. How did you get here anyway?"

"Somebody drove us. But not all the way to the village. The driver was scared."

I nod. The girl has found some raspberries in the garden and pops them in her mouth.

The man watches her from the window. "Are the berries irradiated, too?"

"Do you not know where you are?"

"Yes, yes," he says. "Do I ever. You don't like stupid questions, do you, Baba Dunja?"

I should go home but something keeps me there. I have to really force myself to leave.

"One last question," he calls after me. "Where can you buy something to eat around here?"

I turn around. I think starvation is a relatively gentle way to go, but it's not in my power to decide how death comes to other people.

The man is waiting for an answer. He is not accustomed to waiting. His oily face twitches impatiently.

"Malyschi. Vegetable garden. Stockpiles. Neighbors."

Then I finally go home.

My work taught me that people always and inevitably do what they want to do. They ask for advice, but don't actually have any use for the opinions of others. From every sentence they strain off only what they want to hear. They ignore the rest. I've learned not to offer advice unless someone explicitly asks for it. I've also learned not to ask questions.

I wait until the evening hours to water my cucumbers and tomatoes. Bees buzz around the yellow zucchini blossoms. I watch them, spellbound. For a long time after the reactor I didn't see any bees around here. Various creatures dealt with it differently. The bees just disappeared. I pollinated my tomatoes by hand with a little paintbrush. Perhaps the fact that bees are now crawling around in the calix of these flowers is just the good news Petrow asked for. If I were younger I would shout the news. I decide to write Irina about it. And Laura.

Later I make a cup of tea from fresh raspberry leaves. When I turn away from the kettle I see Jegor sitting there. I feel bad that I can't offer him a tea. It's always nicer to drink tea with someone else. It is perhaps the one thing that with age becomes better to do with company than alone. One time I poured a cup for him out of politeness, but I realized I wasn't doing him any favor by doing that.

Jegor looks at me with his dark eyes. I'm getting self-conscious. I've aged since his death and he could be my son at this point. He doesn't need to undress me with his eyes like that.

After a moment I can't take it any longer. "What are you staring at?"

He leans back. "I love to look at you."

"Do you know any languages other than Russian?"

"Surzhyk."

"That's not a language. It's a dialect. Didn't you learn anything in school?"

"We didn't have any foreign languages in school," he says unperturbed, looking through me. Surely he sees Laura's letter in my sleeve. I'm grateful that he doesn't say anything.

"Have you seen the newcomers?"

He raises an eyebrow. "The guy is an asshole," he says.

I don't contradict him. Even though I don't believe there are good and bad people. I wouldn't know which group I myself would belong to, for instance. When I was young I put so much effort into being a good person that I was dangerous to others. I was very strict with my children so they'd be decent, hardworking citizens. Now I'm sorry I didn't indulge them more. But indulging children was looked down on in our day. People used to say that the only thing you got from indulging your children was coddled good-for-nothings, and I wanted to spare them that. I was particularly strict with Alexej, even though it broke my heart.

"The girl is going to die," says Jegor.

I look up from my teacup. Of course she will. We are all going to die. Some sooner, some later, and a child who moves here certainly won't be around long. Children are frail and delicate. It's the tough, old lumps like Marja and I who hang on forever. No microwaves are going to wear us down.

"He'll kill her with his own hands." Jegor looks out the window knowingly.

"What can he do about her being sick?" Even in death I won't let him get away with it when he acts as though he is the smarter of us two.

"He is doing something about it because he brought her here."

And then I begin to understand what he is getting at because I was thinking the same thing the whole time. "You mean she's not sick?"

In the past he would have spat on the floor. Now he just shrugs his shoulders. "Not yet. But that could change fast."

"But why would a father do something like that?"

"Fathers." Now he spits on the floor after all. "You know everything about fathers. What kind of father was I?"

For the sake of civility, I remain silent. Most women I know would have been better off raising their children on their own rather than constantly stumbling over the boots of their drunken husbands.

But I don't think it's right. Deep in my heart I feel that humans belong in pairs. At least if they have responsibilities. A family is for two. I missed Jegor even while he was alive, no matter what I always claimed. Now he's here and it's too late.

"You know something," I say.

"His wife left him. He wants to teach her a lesson," says Jegor.

I always forget how old I am. I'm constantly surprised by my creaking joints, by how difficult it is to get out of bed each morning, by the unfamiliar puckered face in the scratched mirror. But now, as I cross the main road, actually running, it feels effortless again. It probably couldn't feel more effortless unless I were dead. I yank open the gate, hurry through the garden, and beat my fist against the blue-painted planks of the side of the house.

The man is soon standing in the doorway in jeans and sneakers. A T-shirt with foreign writing on it is stretched across his shoulders.

"What do you want?" He shrinks back from me. I put my foot into the doorway before he can close the door.

"You've brought a healthy child here?"

He tries to shove my foot in the hiking sandal out of the doorway with his sneaker. We grunt like a couple of mating wild boars.

"Have you completely lost your mind?" That's me.

"You should concern yourself with your own sanity."

"Your wife left you, but why drag the little girl into it?"

"Nonsense." He kicks my foot and I stumble backwards, nearly falling over. Jegor is standing behind me but he can't do anything to hold me up.

"You have to leave here right away!" I haven't shouted like this in ages. "She's healthy!"

"Who among us is really healthy?"

He steps out of the house and comes right up to me. I plead with him, saying how sweet his daughter is, that he should go somewhere else with her, that he can jump in front of a train for all I care but that he needs to take the child home, away from here. His face contorts into a grimace. He shoves me, I stagger and grab his T-shirt to steady myself. He swats at my arm. The cloth rips with a dry sound, or maybe it's actually something inside me as his fists land on my ribs. It hurts, but I have no fear of pain. My only fear is of helplessness. But even that can't keep me from saying things that are important to me.

"What do you know anyway?" he grunts as he jabs roughly at my shoulder. Now I really do fall over. I'm lying on the ground, above us the Big Dipper illuminated in the cloudless sky. He kicks me in the side with all his weight, his face looks distorted. His fingers close around my throat. I hear myself wheezing. How quiet two people can be when one is in the process of killing the other.

Jegor stands behind him, crying.

What happens next I don't understand at first. A dry snap out of nowhere. The man, who never introduced himself by name, stands up straight and lurches. For a second he stands there in a contorted, unnatural position. Then he falls to the ground right next to me.

Against my will I suddenly start to moan. When a strong man just falls over like that it's always a fright. My first imperative is to stand up. I roll onto my left side and then onto my stomach. Next I get to my knees and brace myself with my hands. I crawl over to the fallen man.

"Sir, what is with you, sir?"

His face is lying in a pool of blood. There's a hatchet stuck in his skull. I look over at Jegor, who is holding his hands up as if to say: You can see for yourself that I'm unarmed. I kneel there groaning with pain and my gaze wanders slowly through the dark, against which a figure slowly starts to form.

"Petrow," I say. "You swine."

There's a maniacal grin on his face. His eyes look into the distance. I wonder if perhaps he is sleepwalking. Then he shakes himself and tries to help me to my feet, which just causes me more pain.

"Why were you fighting with him, Baba Dunja?"

"I didn't want to have him here."

"Was he misbehaving? Didn't show you respect?"

"You can see for yourself." I stand up and let him kneel down and let him brush the dirt off the hem of my skirt.

"I'm terribly sorry to muck up such a lovely evening, but I'm afraid I've killed him."

I've seen too many wounds in my life to contradict him.

"The question is an easy one," says Petrow. "What shall we do with him?"

"At this point," I say, holding my ribs, the stabbing pain screaming with every breath I take, "the question doesn't concern him."

The girl sits in bed and blinks in the dark. Our dirty faces must have given her a terrible scare. But she's brave. She doesn't cry, she stares at me, now barely blinking. I probably remind her of someone.

"You're going to come with me now, Glascha," I say, trying not to betray my distress. "Your papa's just conked out."

She doesn't ask about him. It's a good sign. Actually a bad sign, but for us at the moment a good one. She crawls out of bed, a proper little girl in a polka-dotted nightgown. Her little suitcase is lying open on the floor, and on her pillow there's a stuffed animal with a long tail.

"Early tomorrow morning it's back home," I say. Actually tonight would be better, but I can't work magic.

I take the girl by the hand. She doesn't notice as she walks past the body of her father, lying like an oblong mound of dirt in the dark. For tonight I'll take her to my place.

Petrow carries her little suitcase and talks to me the whole time. He's making me crazy, because at the same time I feel as if I can see the radiation pressing through the pores in the skin of this child. It allows me to forget my own injuries.

"Aluminum foil," I say loudly. "If anything can help us now, it is aluminum foil."

"Who here has aluminum foil?"

"I do. I have foil."

I do in fact have some, thanks to Irina. She has sent me all sorts of things for the kitchen, practical, German things that we never had in the past. Parchment paper to bake bread on without getting the baking sheet greasy. Silicone forms for baking small cakes, which in the past I had to use rinsed-out jam jars for. And good, strong aluminum foil reinforced in a honeycomb pattern.

"Glascha," I say. "You are going to be surprised."

The girl must have an old soul. She isn't surprised by much. I ask her if she knows what is unusual about our village. She shakes her head. Maybe it's better that way. I've seen people get burns because they imagine they have touched something glowing. If I tell the girl about the radiation she won't survive even a month.

"It's like a game," I say. "You're going to think it's silly, but in exchange you'll stay healthy and grow up to have five kids with a nice man."

She laughs, apparently she finds the image funny. I unpack the aluminum foil, Petrow helps me. In her suitcase Glascha has a pair of tights and a long-sleeved shirt, she has to put those on so that the armor doesn't scratch her tender skin. Then she stretches out her arms and legs and we wrap the silver foil around them. Glascha giggles. I'm thankful for her agreeable nature, that she doesn't cry and she doesn't balk. Even the iodine tablets from my home pharmacy she gulps down without grumbling. If she's always so obedient you almost have to fear for her.

She falls asleep in my bed without complaint after she has tossed and turned in the foil. I lie awake next to her feeling weighed down, breathing shallowly so my ribs don't hurt too badly. I used to sleep like this with Irina and Alexej when they were little and nestled against my body, which back then was quite sizable. They liked that I was so soft and warm. Jegor liked it, too.

The girl breathes as delicately as a bird in my bed, Petrow is swaying in the hammock in his garden, and Jegor haunts his way around the abandoned gardens and bemoans the loss of things he can never bring back.

It's embarrassing, but I have to stick to the truth. Of all

mornings, I slept late on this one. I open my eyes and the bed beside me is empty. If I were to get up hastily I'd have to spend the rest of the week crawling on all fours, and I'm too old for that. A crackling sound directs my gaze. Glascha is rolling old buttons across the wood floor, she must have found them in a drawer. The buttons stop at the bedside carpet. The aluminum foil hangs from her in tatters.

Now I do jump out of bed. For a second the pain pins me back down on the mattress and I suppress a groan.

"You have to watch out for the foil, my little gold piece."

"It got messed up."

"I see that. We'll make you a new set of armor." Now I also have to cough miserably because my throat feels so damaged.

We are just finished with the foil when someone knocks on the door. I quickly wrap a scarf around my neck to hide the strangulation marks. Then I open the door. The Gavrilows are standing there, both with the same look on their faces. Mr. Gavrilow looks as if I have pooped in front of his garden gate.

"Baba Dunja," says Mrs. Gavrilow while her husband peers past her into my sitting room. "We think that you should be the first to know."

I shove Glascha behind my back, as if I could shield her this way from all the evil of this world.

"The newcomer is lying in the garden with a split skull," Mrs. Gavrilow reports precisely and spitefully.

"My papa?" asks Glascha startlingly astutely behind my back.

"No, another person," I answer automatically.

"But where is my papa?"

"He had to make an unexpected trip, dear."

She accepts this. Or, at any rate, she doesn't ask any more questions and gets down on her knees to collect the scattered buttons.

"And what do you expect from me, Lydia Illjinitschna?" In special situations we address each other by first name and father's name. We've never lifted a drink to friendship together.

"There are flies on him already," says Mr. Gavrilow, looking at me reproachfully.

Not ten minutes later they are squatting on my bed drinking the African coffee Irina sent me from Germany. The Gavrilows are at least twenty years younger than I am. And yet they seem to think that the death in the garden is more my concern than theirs. The rationale for this they keep to themselves for a while until Mr. Gavrilow tentatively lets it out of the bag.

"You are sort of like the mayor here."

"Nobody has ever insulted me like that before."

"I understand that you have a lot to do, Baba Dunja, but it's unhygienic."

Ten minutes later my house is so full that I send Glascha out to play. I would like to go with her but everyone is talking at me. Even Lenotschka is there. Scattered among them are the dead, who grimace disgustedly when the living step on their feet. All of them want to tell me that the newcomer is lying in the garden with an axe in his head. All of them look at me and expect me to make him disappear. Along with the flies. And the commotion.

My own head hurts so badly by this point that it feels as if I have an axe in my brain, too. Usually those of us here in Tschernowo leave each other in peace. Sometimes we visit each other, but never all at once. We have an unspoken agreement that everyone takes care of his or her own problems without disturbing the others. For example, I don't wave Laura's letter and shout, "Who can tell me what this says? Can anyone tell the difference between German and English?"

But now there is a collective problem, and there are flies on it.

Petrow turns up at some point as well. Everyone moves aside for him: his apparent proximity to death affords him respect. He wasn't expecting the crush of people and he peers around somewhat intimidated. From the look on his face it's clear that he, too, wants me to decide what to do next. I sigh. My ribs hurt worse and worse, but that's not something I want the others to notice. I press a hand against them as inconspicuously as possible.

"Petrow," I say loudly. "Don't you also tell me there's someone lying in the garden."

Petrow closes his mouth and tries to read my expression.

Sit down with the others and act shocked, I try to tell him with my eyes. I won't betray you. The others have no idea it was you.

The animated chattering continues.

"We have to call an ambulance!"

"A hearse," corrects Petrow shyly.

"We need to go to Malyschi."

"What would we do there? They're all corrupt and drunk."

"I can't manage the hike there."

"Who here is in the best shape?"

"Me, I'm practically dead."

"I've had water in my lungs for five years."

"My heart laughs itself silly if I take more than three steps."

The ones who feel sickest of all are the two rosy-cheeked Gavrilows. Of course. In the end, it emerges that they all consider me the fittest.

"The audacity you all have to suggest an old woman, who already has one foot in the grave, undertake this journey. Don't you have any conscience? I was just in Malyschi and won't manage it a second time."

"All right, Baba Dunja." That's Petrow now. "I'll go. You look really pale. Everyone out, she needs to lie down."

The Gavrilows do in fact make a show of trying to get up from my bed. But then they sit back down. I look at Petrow's translucent face. He almost certainly hasn't eaten anything today, and very little yesterday. His eyes gleam and the few hairs on his head are standing on end. You didn't have to have been a nurse's assistant to see that Petrow wouldn't make it far.

It really will have to be me. I'll take Glascha. If I walk slowly and breathe gently, I might make it. I just need to gather my strength a little, for fifteen minutes at least. But before I can tell everyone, Sidorow's voice quakes through my house.

"One could also call the military police."

He really said it: One could also call the military police. A feeling of awkwardness spreads through the house.

"Perhaps you can phone home like E.T., but us earthlings need a functioning line."

That's Petrow. I can tell from the faces of the others

that as far as they are concerned he is speaking in riddles. Who knows what half-rotted book he's been reading.

"I only wanted to help you idiots." Sidorow's voice wells up, offended. "It won't be long before he stinks to high heaven."

Everyone nods. Nobody wants Sidorow to get upset.

"The sound quality is VERY GOOD!"

"Thank you, Sidorow," I say. "Maybe later."

He slams the door as he leaves, shaking my entire cottage. Someone must have found what was left of my gooseberry vodka, which I keep for medicinal purposes. When the bottle is passed to me it is as good as empty. I look around for a glass but then just pour the rest straight into my mouth from the bottle.

The door suddenly opens and Glascha appears on the threshold in aluminum foil.

"I called Mama," she says loudly, after she has found me.

I shove the empty bottle behind my back, ashamed.

"I told you." Sidorow rocks back and forth behind Glascha like a reed in the wind. Glascha's whole face is lit up.

"I called Mama. I knew the number."

"You are my clever little piece of gold," I say. "Sidorow, I tell you this in all sincerity: I'm already sick to my stomach without your help. Get out of here and don't make the child crazy."

"Mama is picking me up!" says Glascha. "Together with the military police."

I feel during the next few hours that they could be the

last for our village. The Gavrilows have done something sensible for the community for a change and covered the dead man with a tarp. I didn't even know they had one, though I had a feeling their farm was a stockpile of valuable and useful things. The others have scattered and gone back to their own houses and yards, and I'm alone with Glascha and Marja, who has spread out on my bed. I sit on a chair and try to find a position in which my ribs hurt a little less.

"I don't think the foil does anything," says Marja.

"Pffff," I say. "It helps a lot."

"Do you know who did it?" asks Marja.

As long as the child is sitting nearby with her ears perked up I can't risk Marja elaborating on her thoughts to me. I shush her admonishingly.

"I think it was Gavrilow," says Marja, not wishing to understand my warning.

"Stupid woman, a boil on your tongue, what motive would he have?"

"He was afraid that he was going to get robbed."

"You spent too long in the sun, Marja."

"Or it was you. You hunted him down."

I spring out of my chair in shock. But I get dizzy and nearly fall over. Marja doesn't notice, she is working on her fingernails with a file Irina sent me.

"Why would I have done it, Marja?"

"Because he was evil."

"I can't kill everyone who is evil."

"Not everyone, naturally." Marja yawns. "Don't get so upset, I'm not going to snitch on you."

"Neither am I," says Glascha.

If I were ten years younger I would now be very scared. But as it is I'm just tired. I'm waiting for everyone else to hole up in their houses so I can sit undisturbed on the bench outside. I dream of winter: everyone cowering inside and the wind blowing snow against the window. I'm even looking forward to Glascha no longer being here. She's constantly hungry and I won't let her eat vegetables from my garden. I make her gruel with UHT milk I fetched from Sidorow, and mix in the last of my sugar because she won't eat the mush otherwise.

"Your mama will surely be here soon."

"My mama is coming as fast as she can." Glascha presses into my hip and buries her snub nose in the folds of my skirt. "My mama cried on the phone."

"And did you really hear her voice? On that broken phone?"

"It wasn't broken. It just crackled a lot."

I sit on the bench and wait. The others are back in their houses, though noses are pressed against windows and eyes peek through the holes in fences. Only Petrow sways in his hammock as if even the end of the world wouldn't disturb him. I would like to tell him not to worry. Nobody will incriminate him.

You can hear them from far off, and it's obvious that it's more than one vehicle. Soon we see them, and it's three. Out front is a tall black vehicle with thick tires. Behind are two cars belonging to the military police. They stop in a cloud of dust on the main road.

Glascha placidly licks clean her bowl of mush. The driver's-side door of the black vehicle is the first to open. It's the type of car that a man should step out of, not a blonde woman in pants like a man and shoes with high heels. Her hair sticks to her head and her mascara is running.

"Where is she?" she calls heartbreakingly. "Where have you hidden her, you vulture?"

"Glascha," I whisper. "She's crazy, don't look."

"That's my mama." Glascha puts the spoon down on the bench and runs off. The woman falls to her knees, opens her arms, and whimpers like she's been shot. The aluminum foil flutters. The girl hangs on the neck of the woman and I get tears in my eyes.

"What have they done to you?" Glascha's mama begins to rip away the foil.

"Dooooon't," Glascha shrieks, sending chills down my spine. "Don't take it off. Or else I'll drop dead."

Everything blends together. The air shimmers. The soldiers surround the mother and child as if they need to protect them from attack. The woman screams unintelligibly. And she pulls a protective suit out of the trunk of the car and tries to force Glascha into it. I wonder why she herself isn't wearing one if she thinks they work. Intermittently she yells "Germann, Germann, you won't get away with this!"

Germann is not her dog, I assume, it's her husband, who is lying beneath Gavrilow's tarp. And on whom the flies are gathering.

I stand up. My ribs make their presence felt again, a miserable groan sneaks out of me. Very slowly I approach the group. The soldiers look at me. The woman presses Glascha to her chest. Glascha turns and beams at me.

"Drive away, daughter," I say to the woman in pants. "Take your child to safety."

The madness seeps from her eyes and it becomes clear

that she is a woman like any other, and you can talk to her normally.

"You mean," she peers into my eyes as if she hopes to find the answers to all her questions there, "You mean it's not too late?"

"It's never too late," I lie. Why does she have to ask me, of all people?

"You are Baba Dunja, aren't you?"

I nod. She sniffles like a little girl, wipes her face, and pulls something small and rectangular out of her pocket. "May I?" she asks, and before I can answer she presses her cheek to mine and takes a photo of us with her portable telephone. Then she takes Glascha by the hand and goes to the car.

The soldiers call to her and ask what to do about serving the criminal complaint. She waves her hand dismissively. She doesn't ask about her husband. If she wanted to see him I would have a problem. But she has her child back and just wants to leave. I can only welcome this decision. Glascha puts on her seatbelt in the backseat and looks at me as I lean against a tree because my legs have gotten weak. I try to return her smile.

"Let the woman drive off, comrade soldier," I say quietly. "But you, please remain here."

Only later do I realize what a colossal mistake I've made. We should have taken care of the man ourselves. If a dozen lame and infirm people join together, they'd have no trouble making a corpse disappear.

I do my citizenly duty and take the military police to the garden. I stand aside while they lift the tarp. I can see the balefulness in their faces. They would also have preferred it if I had not enlightened them. There are too many of them for us to strike a deal that they didn't see anything.

"Who is the mother of the girl anyway?" I quietly ask the youngest of them, a wispy fellow who fidgets with the fluff on his upper lip.

"You do not want to know," he answers just as quietly. "But believe me, she will not grieve."

That is obvious to me. The ones with grieving looks on their faces are the soldiers. One of them takes photos. Another wraps his arms around himself as if he were freezing. A third shakes his portable phone.

"There's no network here. We have to make a call. Where was the mother called from?"

I take them to Sidorow's house. They enter without knocking. I wouldn't do such a thing and I'm practically his fiancee. Sidorow takes no notice of them; he's snoring on his worn-out ottoman like a sheik. A cable runs from a wall socket to the formerly orange phone, which is sitting on the floor.

The youngest policeman lifts the device and picks up the handset. He holds it to his ear and then passes it on. Presumably his superior, who looks at me furiously.

"Are you trying to yank my chain, old woman?"

He is livid and it looks as if he's going to strike me. But he doesn't after all. Perhaps the soldiers today are different than those in the past, or perhaps he has an old mother or grandmother at home. The young soldier turns the rotary dial, fascinated.

"I would be very grateful, captain, if you would take the dead man with you. The temperature is high and the vermin are multiplying quickly. We don't want disease to break out here."

"As if you were in a sanatorium here. I don't drive a hearse, old woman, in case you haven't noticed. We are going back to Malyschi now." He smiles. "Expect a visit from our colleagues."

It is this smile that sends me back to a time when my heart seldom beat slower than a hundred beats per minute. I'm not a cold-blooded person, never have been. Basically I've always just tried to get by. At times like this I forget that I'm old and no longer need to go anywhere.

It is like I am thirty again and must do everything by myself. Wake up at five in the morning, milk the cows, set a chicken soup to boil, then gruel, put both under a fur coat to stay warm. Collect the eggs in the chicken coop and hard-boil a few for the lunch break. Wake up Irina, she yawns and whines. Wake up Alexej, which is quick and easy, he hops around the house like a rabbit and can only be corralled with great effort. I put their spoons in front of them and check to make sure they eat all their gruel. I don't check their school satchels, there's not enough time. I give them the exact number of coins for school lunch and tell Irina that she should warm up the chicken soup for them later. I don't even have a second to spare to watch them walk down the street.

I pack two hard-boiled eggs in a napkin and stow them in my bag. I run to the bus stop and break a heel along the way. I quickly take off the other shoe and break that heel off. In the little bus to Malyschi I have to stand; an unwashed armpit blocks my view, but I'm a medical professional and will certainly be confronted with worse smells during the course of the day. Once I've arrived at the city's emergency ward, I put on my white hospital smock. From that point on I am a machine that bandages wounds, removes splinters, splints a broken leg, comforts a vomiting child, and wraps a tape measure around a pregnant woman's belly. The doctor insists it must be twins and I argue with him because I don't think that's the case. The baby will weigh nearly five kilos when it is born, it's a boy.

At lunch I eat my eggs with a piece of bread and wash it down with kvass that the doctor has brought in a plastic bag from a street merchant. I think about Irina and Alexej and wonder whether they did everything properly today. I can't call them because we have no phone at home. We are on the waiting list for a phone line, but it's expected to take at least another five years. But the children know how they can reach me at work, and I cringe every time the phone rings here. The device was similar to Sidorow's, and I would have cut off a finger to have one like it at home.

In the bathroom I wash my hands and put on lipstick. A worn-out woman with drooping eyelids looks out at me from the mirror. I feel ancient and look it, too. I haven't seen Jegor for three days and have no idea where he is hiding. I take off my shoes, sit on the lid of the toilet, and do some vein exercises that I read about in *Woman Farmer*.

When I come to, it is ten at night. The children are sleeping back to back in the big bed, and I pull their notebooks out of their satchels and correct their homework. The dishes are washed, the socks are stuffed. I'm no good at homework, but I do my best. I go to the kitchen and drink a glass of tap water. It tastes salty because my tears are dropping into the glass. I'm just a woman like millions of others and still so unhappy, I'm an idiot.

"Tell me what I should do," Petrow demands, jarring

me from my reverie. "I'm full of nervous energy." As proof he hoists his scrawny little arms and balls his bony fists. "Shall we burn him like the Indians do?"

"Where do you get such garbage in your head?" He has succeeded in perking me up, but I don't show it. "Nobody will come to get him. We have to dig him a grave."

"We're not qualified. But I'm with you." He wanders off and returns with a shovel that looks suspiciously like one that belongs to the Gavrilows.

We wait until the sun isn't beating down and then get started. Or rather, Petrow does, beginning to dig. He has overestimated himself. After every scoop he has to catch his breath for a few seconds, and after five he has to take a break for a few minutes. But he keeps going. He is a man, so I can't say anything. I bring him hot water with mint.

"I'd rather have a cola with ice cubes," he groans, propping himself up on the shovel.

"Cold chemicals in the heat will kill you," I say.

Every now and again he sets himself down in the grass, at which point I pick up the shovel and ignore the pain in my ribs. I'm surprised how difficult it is. The fact that I'm apparently weaker than the infirm Petrow frightens me, but I don't think about it for long. The rich, reddish-brown dirt piles up in puny molehills.

"You are not allowed to say that we cannot do it. You have to believe in us," says Petrow, but I ignore his nonsense.

Flies buzz above the tarp. Time is working against us. Sweat runs down our faces, but the molehills barely get bigger. I sit down next to Petrow and close my eyes.

When I open them again I see Marja shoveling.

I have to say, she is of a completely different caliber. I've never seen her work before, and I didn't know what I was missing. Her huge white body proves strong. She shovels like a backhoe and is barely breathing hard. It must be all the pills she gulps down daily, or her iron constitution that even the pills can't weaken.

Petrow and I watch speechlessly. Marja doesn't look at us. She concentrates on shoveling. The dirt flies into our faces. She pauses only to wipe her brow. Her round cheeks have reddened and her braids are coming undone. She could be the featured soloist in a folk-dancing troupe.

Maybe she once was, who knows.

When she takes a break on the grass next to us, Petrow tries to stand up again. He can't. He makes a few jokes about it, that we might as well dig a grave for him while we're at it, but Marja ignores him. She reaches out for some juicy burdock leaves, rips a few off with a precise motion, and puts one on her forehead and two smaller ones on her cheeks.

Soon Sidorow takes up the shovel. He looks over at me proudly but a moment later nearly falls into the hole. Marja takes the shovel from him. He props himself up on his cane and watches her with a look that betrays the fact that he hasn't given up on finding a good match.

Marja takes off her wool jacket. Her upper arms are round and quiver like jelly. The flesh is so pink that you want to bite into it. Mr. Gavrilow comes and watches silently. Marja indulges him. At some point she takes off her kneesocks and puts her shoes back on. Sidorow wipes his face. Gavrilow gulps loudly. Only Petrow keeps his eyes closed.

Marja shovels with a victorious smile on her face. She is

now standing in a knee-deep pit. She shakes her head like a wild horse and then hands the shovel to Gavrilow.

Mr. Gavrilow, whom I have never seen doing anything that doesn't directly and exclusively benefit him, takes the shovel. His hand brushes Marja's. She shows her teeth, her laugh sounds fake in my ears. The fact that she's younger than I am does not make her a spring chicken. Gavrilow doesn't seem to notice. Under Marja's watchful eye, he begins to dig wildly, furiously, like an anteater.

His rhythmic grunts spur Mrs. Gavrilow into action. I fear that he's earned himself a smack on the head later. But for now, Gavrilow is king of the pit and we are his audience. We breathe in unison. The mounds of earth grow.

Jegor comes, too. I want to deflect his attention toward Marja—he always knew when there was something about a woman to look at—but he fixates on me the way a cat fixates on a bottle of valerian. Other dead gather as well. Glascha's father isn't one of them; I'm happy about that. His body lies under the tarp and his blood has seeped into our earth.

It is getting dark by the time Gavrilow retrieves from his house a tattered bedsheet splattered with pale stains. I pull the tarp away. A swarm of flies rises. Marja turns away and throws up in the raspberries.

Pooling our strength we wrap Glascha's father in the sheet, tie it head and foot, and pull him into the grave. We all push and pull together. Our hands brush one another in the silence that is broken only by the scraping sound and our breathing. The body lands with a thump in its new bed.

Filling the hole back in goes more quickly, even though

we are tired. When everyone has left, I stomp the soil smooth on top. My bones feel hollow from fatigue.

Nothing in the world is as horrible as being young. It's okay as a child. If you're lucky there are people to look after you. But from sixteen on it gets harsh. You're really still a child, but everyone just sees you as an adult who is easier to step on than one who is older and more experienced. Nobody wants to protect you anymore. New responsibilities are constantly foisted upon you. Nobody asks you whether you understand the latest thing you are supposed to do.

It really gets bad after marriage. Suddenly you are responsible not only for yourself but for others, and there are always more and more who wish to ride on your back. In your heart, though, you are still the child you always were and will remain for a long time. If you are lucky you'll be half-mature by the time you get old. Only then are you in a position to be able feel sympathy for those who are young. Until then you begrudge them for whatever reason.

Those are the things that go through my head when I think about Irina and Laura.

I want to send Irina a letter. She complains that I don't write often enough. I know that in reality she doesn't sit around waiting for my letters. But she wants me to think that she cares about me. She's also afraid that I'm bored, and writing a long letter is a peaceful and sensible activity. She doesn't believe me when I say that I don't even know what it means to be bored. She is a good daughter and wants confirmation from me that she is paying sufficient attention to me. Since Alexej took off to the other side of the globe, she's my closest kin, geographically speaking as well. She must live with a permanently bad conscience.

So I sit down at the kitchen table, grab my school-style graph-paper notebook and a pen, and start to write. I don't touch the new pink paper, that's for Laura. Irina doesn't care for pink.

My dear daughter Irina, I write, *my dear son-in-law Robert, and my beloved only grandchild, Laura. Baba Dunja greets you warmly from the village of Tschernowo by Malyschi. How are you all? I am well, even though I can tell I'm no longer 82 anymore. But for my advanced age, I am very content. I am particularly pleased with the hiking sandals that you, Irina, sent me from Germany. You are always so good at picking out the right size for me. Since I've been wearing them my feet hurt much less.*

I went to Malyschi this week and retrieved the new letters and packages. Much gratitude to you all. I particularly appreciate the vanilla sugar, which I use sparingly, and the reading lens. Though actually I'm still quite satisfied with my eyes. When I was your age, Irina, I thought I would soon go blind. It still hasn't happened.

The weather is summery, early in the morning it's 60 degrees or so, and by noontime the thermometer pushes toward 90. It's not always easy to bear, especially when evening temperatures only cool down to the mid-70s and, as I mentioned, don't reach the 60s, which I find most comfortable, until the early morning.

The mood here in Tschernowo is very good. I often have my neighbor Marja over for coffee, which you, Irina, sent.

I've told you about her. She's not too clever but she's good-natured. She's younger than I am.

I lean back and think. I feel obligated to tell Irina something about yesterday, but carefully, so she doesn't get upset.

This week something unusual took place. We gained two new residents, but they were unable to stay. Life in Tschernowo is very nice, but it's not suitable for everyone.

I want to say something to Robert, too. I've never seen Irina's husband, but I want to demonstrate my respect for him.

I know that you have a lot to do as a family. Laura will graduate soon and will turn eighteen, and you, Irina and Robert, work so much at the hospital. I am sure that you do a lot for people through your work and that they are thankful to have you.

Irina has never told me much about Robert. The last time she sent me a photo with him in it was probably ten years ago. He was balding and had a big nose. But a husband needn't be handsome. Jegor was, but what good was it to me?

Irina, I think often about your father. He had his failings, but he was a good man.

I know that you sometimes worry about me. You needn't. I am getting by very well, and I feel very much at ease. I hope that you are taking good care of yourselves.

I turn the page over. My pen marks have pressed through the back of the paper. I've already written a lot. Irina will be comforted.

I've written so much already. Please forgive me for taking so much of your time.

Fond greetings from Tschernowo, your Baba Dunja.

The letter needs to be mailed. But I won't make it to Malyschi in the next few days. I need to rest, for at least two weeks. If it were me, I wouldn't return to Malyschi for the rest of the summer. I'd like to sit on the bench and stare at the clouds and once in a while exchange a word with Marja.

In reality I rarely sit on the bench. And most times when I do I get up almost immediately to go sweep the floor, beat the rugs, clean the pots with sand, or scrape the rust off the teakettle. Weeds are sprouting green and luscious, I rip them out, and when I straighten up again I see black. It doesn't make me afraid, I just wait for my vision to clear.

The haze before my eyes dissipates, and I see the face of a serious little girl with pale blonde hair. My beloved granddaughter Laura, whom I have never met and who has written me a letter that I can't read.

For a moment I feel a sense of horror. I think that Laura has come to Tschernowo as a ghost. But it's just the heat and my old veins. Laura is at home in Germany. She is safe. I didn't mention in my letter to Irina that Laura wrote me. I don't actually know anything about Laura. The things that Irina writes about her don't give a clue about what Laura is like as a person. Laura is in first grade, Laura transferred into fifth grade, Laura will graduate this year. It doesn't tell you anything.

I don't even know what language she wrote her letter in and why. Maybe she needs help and I can't do anything for her. It breaks my heart.

Her reality, which I know nothing about, now stands alongside Irina's, which I can really only guess at.

That Irina is a good woman I believe deeply and firmly. She wears a white lab coat. On her chest pocket, her name is embroidered, a German one. The name of her husband. I have a photo of her in a lab coat like that, it's hanging next to the photos of Laura.

Irina competes with men, men who have a lot more muscle than she. Unlike me, she is a doctor. I know what that means. My superiors were doctors. They ruled over me, or acted like they did, though often they left me to my own devices because it saved them a lot of work. Some insisted on meddling in everything and dictating your every move. Some thought they knew everything. A few drank liquor in the examination room or locked themselves in the supply closet with one of the female medics. I knew about it but I never said anything; when it happened I did my own work and that of the doctor and medic, and I did it well. And through it all I had to be sure not to damage the men's egos.

Irina told me that she doesn't have the same problem. But I don't believe her.

When Irina comes to visit me, it's never just about me. An old woman is not sufficient justification for a trip like that. She leads groups of sick children from our region back to Germany, farms them out to families, and lets them have three weeks of vacation with fresh air and no radiation. She examines them in her hospital and sends them to the zoo and the pool accompanied by volunteers. That's my daughter. After three weeks the children are sent back, sunburned and with a little more flesh on their bones.

I pull out Laura's letter and look at the words, but I can't even guess at what it says.

Later I take a stroll through the village to look in on Petrow. I have two cucumbers and three peaches along with me. The cucumbers are from my garden, the peaches I plucked from an abandoned property. The peach tree stands buckled over and knotted, straining under the weight of the fruit. It has been a bountiful year: apricots, cherries, apples—all the trees are bearing more fruit than ever before.

I think of the lab technicians who marched into our village and wanted to take samples of our crops. Sidorow proudly gave them his monster zucchini, Lenotschka handed them eggs over her fence, Marja yelled derisively, "Of course, I'll get up right away and milk my goat for you, anything else?" and I shrugged my shoulders and left the masked figures, saying they could gather up whatever they wanted. They needed to do their work, after all. The first time they came I opened a jar of pickled mushrooms for them because I wanted to treat them like guests. They forked a mushroom and stuck it into a container with a screw-top. They handled my tomatoes with rubber gloves. During their next visit I left my preserves on my shelf.

From the squeak of the hammock I can tell that Petrow is still in the land of the living. He is lying there like a giant grasshopper, his dark, bulging eyes looking at me. I approach him and put the fruit in his lap.

He waves a book he has in his hand. "Have you ever read Castaneda, Baba Dunja?"

"No." I sit down on a chair with a sawed-off back that he keeps in the yard and fold my hands.

"You're not much of a reader, isn't that right?"

"I'm sorry?"

"You have never read much, I asked," he yells, even though I can hear him very well.

"We didn't have any books at home. Magazines maybe. And reference books, for work. Textbooks during my training. I sent them all to Irina when she began to study medicine."

"All of them? Don't you have any left?"

"No, they're all gone."

"And what if you have to look something up here?"

"I don't need to look anything up. Whatever I need I already know."

"Funny. For me it's the other way around." He tosses the book carelessly to the ground. "And don't you get bored without any books?"

"I don't get bored. I always have work to do."

"You are a wonder, Baba Dunja."

I don't respond.

"Have you ever heard of the Internet?"

"I've heard of it." And it's true, I have. "But I've never seen it."

"Where would you. We live in the Stone Age here. Instead we have a ghost telephone that works once a year and nobody can explain why."

"You can't explain everything in life."

"From anyone else that would be an unbearably banal statement."

That's how Petrow talks. He's a man who needs books the way an alcoholic needs liquor. When he doesn't have enough to read he's insufferable. And he never has enough. Tschernowo doesn't have a public library, and he's already devoured everything here, right down to instruction manuals that are older than he is.

"I wonder if the phone will work when my time is up."

"We'll see."

"Nothing rattles you, does it, Baba Dunja?"

I don't answer. Laura's letter is burning against my skin. It's giving me abrasions. Petrow looks at me intently.

"You sometimes talk about your daughter, but why never about your son?"

"He's even farther away. In America."

"America is big. Where exactly?"

"On the coast. It's warm and oranges grow there."

"Florida? Or California?"

"I don't know."

"Why doesn't he ever write to you?"

"He sends me a card every Christmas. American Christmas. He doesn't like women."

Petrow takes half a second to digest this.

"And because of that you have disowned him?"

"I haven't disowned anyone. But it's good that he's no longer here."

"Do you miss him?" He looks at me searchingly.

I look down at the ground. The dirt on Petrow's property is sandier than elsewhere. It absorbs a lot of water. Petrow's voice is like a rustle in the wind. He talks about all the places he's been. That he, too, lived in America, in New York and California. That he has traveled the world. That there are people who not only eat no meat but no milk and no eggs, and don't buy leather shoes because of the animals. These are things that must come out of him again and again, things I already know. He talks like a broken radio receiver. But he is still here, and he bites off half of one of the cucumbers I brought over.

"So you can speak English, then, Petrow?"

"Of course I can speak English."

Laura's letter throbs beneath my sleeve.

"And you know other languages, too?"

"Others, too."

It would be so easy to ask him. It's not that I have anything against Petrow. I just don't trust him or anyone else.

"What are you thinking?" he asks, reaching for a peach.

"I'm thinking that you are very different from me."

"If at some point you are no longer here, Baba Dunja, Tschernowo will disappear."

"I don't believe that."

He spits out the peach pit and follows its trajectory with his eyes.

"Do you think a new peach true will grow out of that?"

"No. Peaches are usually propagated with cuttings."

"I mean, will this area forget one day what has been done to it? In a hundred or two hundred years? Will people live here and be happy and carefree? Like before?"

"What do you know about what it was like here before?"

It's possible that he is a little offended. He is the only one here who talks like that, and I don't think it's right. It's the type of thing written in the papers and has nothing to do with those of us here in Tschernowo.

"Thanks for the cucumbers and peaches," he calls after me when I've taken my leave.

I realize that it takes me a few minutes longer than usual to make my way back along the main road. As I pass the garden with the grave I notice that someone has strewn rose petals on top of the newly filled spot.

The grief hits me without warning and, as always, at an inopportune time. The worries concentrate behind my forehead and I can no longer think straight. It's moments like these that take me back to a life that I no longer have. A talk with Petrow is always a good trigger. He asks questions that go straight to the heart and that you have no answer for.

During the first year in Tschernowo I was asked many questions. The most difficult came from Irina. The most inane from the reporters. They followed me at every turn, wrapped up like astronauts in their radiation suits. Baba Dunja, they shouted agitatedly, what message are you trying to send? How will you survive in a place where there is no longer any life? Will you allow your family to visit you? What are your blood counts? Have you had your thyroid checked? Who will you allow to move into your village?

I don't know if they ever understood that it isn't my village. I tried to talk to them, showed them my house and garden, the other houses that were empty then. That, too, was a mistake, I should have turned away from the cameras and closed the door in their faces. But I was raised differently, and that outweighed decades of professional experience as a nurse's assistant.

"You shouldn't have told them that you love this land," Petrow had informed me later. "They will construe it as a provocation, as a purposeful trivialization of the reactor disaster. They will hate you for it, for letting yourself be exploited."

"Yes, should I have told them that in reality I don't care whether I die a day sooner or a day later?"

"Maybe you should have," Petrow said.

Laura's letter burns furiously at my soul. It's too much for me to deal with alone. I must find a way to read it.

The next morning I sit on the bench in front of my house with heavy feet and a heavy head. The cat skulks around me. It is steadily gaining weight, I watch as it catches spiders one after the next and giddily destroys their webs. One shouldn't think that animals are any better than people. The cat jumps onto my shoulder and licks my ear with its rough tongue.

"I don't like the way you look today," says Marja. I didn't hear her coming. She's standing there with her big body, her broad feet in worn-out slippers, her unkempt golden hair. She's wearing her greasy bathrobe and beneath that a negligee that's faded to gray from being washed so many times.

"Why don't you get dressed?" I ask sternly.

"I am dressed."

"Other people live here, too. Men. You shouldn't walk around like that."

"Do you think Gavrilow could rape me? Move over." She shoves me to the end of the bench with her massive rear end.

"Sidorow asked for my hand," she says without looking at me.

"Congratulations."

"I told him I needed to think about it."

"Why string along a decent man?"

"It's not the sort of thing to enter into lightly."

I nod and straighten the kerchief on my head. The heat of her body ensures that sweat begins to trickle down my right side.

"I've been without a man for a while now," Marja continues and then looks at me from the side, as if anticipating a reaction.

"You're no less lonely when you have a man. And what's worse, you have to take care of him."

She whistles through her teeth like a schoolboy. "Would you be angry with me if I said yes?"

My ribs still hurt so badly that I can't turn to her. "Why would I be angry with you? I'd be happy for you."

"Ach, I don't know." She reaches for the seam of her washed-out nightgown and wipes her nose. "There are enough reasons to be angry with me."

"Not at all. He is a very old man but noble of heart. You are a beautiful woman. You make a good pair."

Out of the corner of my eye, I can see her blushing.

That night I dream that my cat gets married to the dead rooster Konstantin.

News travels fast in any village. In ours you need only think something and the neighbors already know. The first one to turn up at my door is Sidorow.

"Congratulations," I say, cautiously, because something in me refuses to believe this development.

"Thank you." He tries to kiss my hand but I take it away from him and tell him he should save his gallantry for his fiancée.

He begins a long speech, loses his train of thought, stops, confused, and then starts again from the beginning. I listen intensely. At some point I realize that he is worried about fulfilling his marital duties.

"You should have thought about that," I say mercilessly. He blinks. He could almost make you feel bad, but old men who seek younger women should consider in advance what they are getting themselves into.

"I wanted it to be you," spills out of him, but I don't want to talk about it, it seems rude to Marja.

He leaves, his back more hunched than usual. I bet his rabbit heart is galloping wildly.

Next, surprisingly, comes Mrs. Gavrilow. She sits down on my chair and says she has heard something. Her way of beating around the bush gets me worked up.

"You heard right," I say. "We will soon celebrate a wedding here in Tschernowo."

"But isn't it somehow immoral?"

"The engaged parties are both of age."

"The question of age is exactly what I wanted to get at."

"The law doesn't bar anyone from marrying after they reach a certain age."

"But where will they live?"

"Why are you asking me, Lydia Iljinitschna? I'm not the mother-in-law. The engaged couple has plenty of square meters of space at their disposal."

Suddenly Mrs. Gavrilow roars with laughter, and the tension in her face dissipates.

"Ach, it's fine with me. At least she'll be out of the way.

I look at her. Marja's strange words about being raped by Gavrilow come back to me. Marja is not a woman who places any value in being handled delicately. And Mrs. Gavrilow is anything but stupid. Perhaps she can even speak German.

"God help him," she says, with schadenfreude in her smile.

A little later Petrow comes by and, before he even enters the house, recites a love poem. And then another. By the third I've had enough.

"What do you want?"

"We're going to celebrate a wedding, and if things keep going like this we will soon hear the patter of tiny feet."

"Then the sky really would fall."

"Isn't it all wonderful, Baba Dunja?"

I answer with a look that makes him cringe. I'm not sure which of his moods bothers me more.

"Okay," he says. "You don't think it's wonderful. You're jealous."

"Not me," I say. "But some here in Tschernowo will be able to sleep better as a result."

Petrow has to sit down as his strength is waning. The skin of his face is waxy and clings to his skull. It looks as if it might rip if Petrow were to smile too broadly.

"You need to eat something," I say. "Otherwise you'll lose your strength too quickly."

"Apparently, there's someone in India who subsists on sunrays."

Petrow stands up. He takes a few steps and then falls onto my bed. I'm actually not thrilled that my bed is now communal property that anyone who happens to stop by feels free to sit on without asking. But if I shoo him off it he'll fall flat on the floor. They've already removed quite a few of his organs; it's a wonder that he's still able to be such a bother.

"I'm sure I'll cry at the wedding," he calls from my bed as I leave my house. "I get more sentimental every day, have you noticed?"

What I would never trade for running water and a telephone in Tschernowo is the matter of time. Here there is no time. There are no deadlines and no appointments. In essence, our daily routine is a sort of game. We are reenacting what people normally do. Nobody expects anything of us. We don't have to get up in the morning or go to bed at night. For all anyone cares, we could do it the other way around. We imitate daily life the same way children do with dolls, or when they're playing store.

At times we forget that there is another world where the clocks move faster and everyone is plagued by horrible fear of the earth that feeds us. This fear is deeply rooted in the other people, and interactions with us bring it to the surface.

Seventeen and a half years ago I dialed Irina's German phone number, which with the country code and area code was very long. She hadn't been reachable by phone for a few months prior to that. She hadn't written me anything either. I had a feeling that it meant something, but I didn't know exactly what. I still lived in Malyschi then, regularly bought five-minute phone cards, stood in line at the international phone booth, waited to be connected, and listened to the outgoing message in German on her answering machine. I always hung up immediately in the firm belief that Irina would pick up the phone at some stage. If something truly awful had happened I would have heard about it already. She would have made sure of that.

And one day she did in fact pick up the phone and said, "Mother, it's good that you called. I wanted to tell you something. You have a grandchild. She is eleven days old and healthy. Her name is Laura."

And I asked: "Are you sure?"

"Of course I'm sure, I named her."

"I don't mean the name."

"You can never be sure. But I did count the fingers and toes." She laughed.

A cry rang out in the background. It sounded like a kitten whose tail had gotten pinched.

"It's a great joy," I said. "Go to your daughter. I'll call you another time."

I didn't call for a while. I knew what it was like when you first had a baby, you don't have a lot of time to talk. I sent Irina a letter in which I remembered what she herself had been like as a baby, and I began to save money. Irina wrote back: *Forgive me, Mother, for not telling you about the pregnancy beforehand. I wanted to wait for the birth.*

She included a photo of a suckling baby with a giant pacifier in its mouth.

I knew exactly what she meant.

When Laura was three, Irina came for the first time to take sick children to Germany. She didn't have Laura with her.

I didn't ask her a single time when I could see my grandchild. I didn't ask why she never brought Laura with her to see her old homeland. I know the answer. I wouldn't want Irina to feel bad about it. She invited me several times to come to Germany, she suggested she could pick me up and take me back. It sounded so easy when she said it. But I don't have any experience with travel. In my entire life I never made it beyond Malyschi.

I regret not taking Irina up on her invitation. When Laura was younger I didn't have the heart to do it. I didn't want to impose on Irina's family. Now I'm too old. The walk to the bus station, the bus ride, and then another bus to the airport, the airplane, the drive to Irina's, I couldn't make it anymore.

And besides, I know that I give off radiation just like the ground and everything that comes out of it. Shortly after the reactor I, like many others, took part in studies— I went to the hospital in Malyschi, sat on a chair, told them my name and birthday while the meter next to me clattered and a nurse's assistant recorded the readings in a notebook. A biologist explained to me later that the stuff was stuck in my bones and gave off radiation around me so that I was myself like a little reactor.

The strawberries and huckleberries in our woods give off radiation, too, as do the porcinis and the birch bolete mushrooms that we gather in autumn, and the meat of the rabbits and deer that Gavrilow sometimes shoots. No outsiders will touch any of it, the most they will do is take samples for their research, but it seems like such a shame to us to put it to that purpose.

Sometimes I think that I owe my long life to the good air and the freshly tapped birch sap I drink early each year. I go into the woods with pickling jars and take the time to find birch trees that seem strong and willing to give me a bit of their sap. I find it barbaric to injure a tree again and again or to take too much sap at one time the way some people do in areas that enjoy a much better reputation than ours. Birch sap sells for a lot, and nobody cares about the scarred, desiccated trees. Me on the other hand, I carefully bore through the bark and insert a tiny capillary tube, hold a jar beneath it, and secure it. The elixir trickles out drop by drop, and when I go back and pick up the jars days later, I tend to the wounded spot with the same care I used to show my patients.

I taught Irina and Alexej that, too: don't destroy anything if it isn't necessary. It's difficult to repair things and something is always lost forever. The village children had a better feeling for it than the summer holiday children who came out from the city. More than once I saw Irina smack their hands when they impatiently plucked an unripe berry or heedlessly pulled a mushroom from the ground only to throw it back down.

I offer the valuable birch sap only to guests who are particularly important to me. I had become fond of the biologist and handed him a glass of the translucent liquid.

"Are you trying to kill me?" He shook his head, laughing.

I love this land, but sometimes I'm glad that my children aren't here anymore.

I knock on Marja's door, a gesture she purposefully neglects when she comes to my place because she mistakenly believes that I have nothing to hide.

She yells for me to come in. She is sitting on her bed and has her long, golden hair down, combing it like an overripe Rapunzel.

"So, bride," I say, "are you getting excited?"

"I've never been a bride," she moans.

"I thought you were married before?"

"Ach," she says, waving her hand dismissively, "that doesn't count. That was a hundred years ago. I don't know what I should wear."

"What are you two going to do with your houses?"

"What do you expect us to do? We'll both keep our own."

"You're not going to sleep together?"

"A boil upon your tongue."

"Why are you getting married then?" I sit down next to her. The mattress is very soft and sags precariously beneath our weight. Marja cries out and grabs me. We have never sat together on her bed, only on mine, which holds up better.

"Let go of me," I sniff. "What has gotten into you, stupid woman, let go of me and help me stand up."

"I'm trying," she whines, but with every movement we are just pressed closer together by the buckling mattress.

When it cracks, I feel as if salvation is at hand. The bed collapses and Marja and I land among the covers on the floor. I crawl out of the mountain of covers, brace myself against the wall, and stand up.

Marja sits between the pillows and sobs.

"Now I don't have a bed anymore."

"But you have a husband who will build you a new one."

"Him? Haven't you seen him?"

"Demand it before you give him a yes."

She runs her hand over her face. "You always have such good ideas. Without you we'd all be done for."

"Don't you start now, too."

Marja looks at me sadly. "I want you to marry us."

When earlier I mentioned the sense of time here, this is what I was getting at: barely aware of what's happening, I'm standing on a lawn, next to me a long, covered table, and in front of me a buxom woman and an old man who looks more like a withered tree than a person.

Behind me stand the village residents. Only Petrow is seated because he is too weak. The others are on their feet. Between the living roam the dead, who seem quite curious. Jegor is directly behind me and looks over my shoulder.

Sidorow built a bed for Marja, an unbelievable bed. Nobody can figure out how he did it. He sawed a tree trunk into four pieces and then, on top, he laid planks he ripped off his shed. Everything secured with lots of nails. Marja's mattress, pillows, and covers went over that. It is a giant, wide bed, the biggest I've ever seen. Marja can sleep well now. She assured me of that when she proudly showed me the bed.

"See what a marriage is good for?" It sounded like she was bragging.

"I never denied it."

"Why are you laughing then?"

"I'm not laughing, Marja. I'm happy for you."

For the wedding Marja wears her lace nightgown,

which is nearly white and also allows her to show off her abundant body. On her shoulders is a black scarf with roses. She has braided her hair and coiled the braids on top of her head in a way that would let her run for parliament. A lace curtain serves as her veil. And flowers, everywhere flowers. Cornflowers in her hair and Sweet William on her nightgown and a dog rose in Sidorow's lapel.

Sidorow's knees tremble and he looks even smaller than he usually does, he props himself up on his cane with his last ounce of strength. The knuckles on his hand protrude, white. But his face is contorted into a victor's grin. You could also confuse it with an expression caused by a death spasm. He is well dressed, moth-eaten gray pinstripe pants and a shirt with a colorful zigzag pattern.

The bridal pair stands before me and looks at me expectantly. Now it's up to me to say something appropriately festive. I'm also dressed up in order to show my respect to the two of them, I'm in a long skirt and a silk blouse, the scarf on my head is freshly washed, and my neck is decorated with a necklace of big, colorful wooden beads.

The tattoo on my hand starts to itch again. I try to remember what the registrar said at my wedding to Jegor. But I can't think of it. Then I think of other weddings I've been to as a guest or witness. That in turn reminds me of the fact that I wasn't at Irina's wedding.

The wedding of my cousin pops into my head, I must have been in my forties, and one sentence in particular that struck me. "Be good to each other" is how the overtired registrar had sent my cousin and her future husband on their way, no more and no less; dozens of couples waited every Saturday at the registrar's office, and a lot of mothers-in-law got aggressive in the hallway. Those words stayed with me for a long time. Though I was already married and a mother at that point.

Much later I saw people on television get married in a church, I even saw a royal wedding. These days a lot of young people get married in churches here in our country, too. Back then you wouldn't have been able to go to work anymore if you did that.

"Give me your hands," I say, and they reach out their paws willingly, Marja's soft and doughy and Sidorow's as dry as a bird's claw. I take them and place them on top of each other. Marja has donated two rings that she dug out of her stockpile.

I hand them to the bridal pair. Sidorow slides the thick ring with glittering stone onto Marja's finger, the finger is too big, Marja grits her teeth. Success. Next Sidorow gets his, but his finger is too bony and the little ring dangles from it. Sidorow makes a fist to keep it from falling off.

"Be good to each other," I say. Marja looks at me with wide eyes, like I'm giving the Sermon on the Mount. "You are now man and wife."

I can tell Marja's pulse is racing. I can't detect anything from Sidorow, his skin is cold and dry. Again a sense of expectation hangs in the air.

"Can you remember?" I whisper to Jegor. "Can you remember what comes next?"

"Bless them," he murmurs in my ear. "And don't forget the kiss."

He can't be serious, I think, these are old people, and I have some decency. But they are still looking as if they are waiting for something in particular, and I sigh loudly.

"I congratulate you, and I . . . bless you," I say, and

Marja's eyes begin to glimmer. "And, if you really want to . . . I would like to say . . . Sidorow, you may now kiss the bride."

We have never done anything together as a village community. We even moved in on our own; first me, then the others. I greeted them, showed them the houses, and gave them some of my tomato crop. But we were not a community; everyone was happy to be left in peace. We have no practice sitting around a common table. Now we are doing it.

A large table has been set up in Marja's garden and covered with multiple bedsheets. Lenotschka scattered rose petals on the sheets. We rounded up utensils from the whole village. In the middle of the table sit: a steaming teakettle with peppermint leaves swimming in it. A plate of fresh cucumbers and a plate of pickles. Tomatoes, cut into slices. Bushels of herbs. Hard-boiled eggs. A semolina cake with cherries that I baked. Two roasted chickens that Lenotschka sacrificed and that everyone is eyeing as if we were starving. And a few bottles of berry wine from Sidorow's shed.

You can't really say the atmosphere is raucous. But there is atmosphere. Marja has removed her veil but the flowers still hang in her hair. Her cheeks are flushed with heat, wine, and bashfulness. Uncharacteristically, she doesn't talk much. She looks from one person to the next and every now and again her gaze lingers on me as if she were trying to send me a message.

Sidorow is talking with Mr. Gavrilow. Everyone bets they are telling dirty jokes. Anger flashes across Mrs. Gavrilow's face but she keeps breaking into snorting laughter. Petrow is unusually quiet and stares incessantly at Lenotschka as if he has never seen her before. Then they move toward each other.

The dead rooster Konstantin jumps into Marja's lap and she doesn't even notice. Konstantin pecks at her puffy arm. The goat chews on her nightgown from the other side.

I make sure the glasses get refilled and that everyone has something on their plate. And I have the feeling that someone is watching us. If I were religious I would say it was God. But God was abolished from our land when I was little and I haven't managed to get him back. There were no icons in my parents' house and we didn't pray. Unlike many others, I did not get baptized in the nineties because I found it too ridiculous as an adult to be dipped in a trough and have scented smoke wafted into my face. Though I am definitely of the opinion that Jesus Christ was a decent man, with all that you hear about him.

I take a sip of wine. The fruity sweetness masks its strength. My head starts to get hazy. I see Jegor's face before me. Sit down, I say. I forgive you.

"What are you babbling about?" Marja leans over and wraps her arms around me.

She smells like grass and sweat. My Marja, whom I took care of when she was laid up for a week in bed with a burning fever. I used up the last of my vodka to rub her with it. She smelled like an emergency room doctor on New Year's Eve. When she broke out in a sweat I washed her. It was different from when I was a nurse's assistant. No matter how much training and experience you have, sometimes you still cannot help marveling like a child at a body like that.

A distant buzz presses into my ear. The rooster Konstantin flaps his wings. Leotschka slides out of Petrow's lap and her eyes fill with fear. Marja lets go of me. I stand up and shade my eyes with my hand.

Dust clouds are moving toward us. I blink again and suddenly I can see that they are the blue and white vehicles of the military police. They are bouncing down the main road. The driver's-side doors open at the same time, armed men in white radiation suits get out.

A shot rings out and a bottle of berry wine bursts into a thousand pieces. Mrs. Gavrilow lets out a high-pitched, ear-splitting scream. The men yell orders at us but it's as if I'm deaf and I can't understand the words. The others at the table apparently can't either. Only Sidorow stands up slowly and raises his hands.

That's when I realize how old I am. Not because of the pain or the fat legs and heavy feet. But because it takes me so long to comprehend the situation. Admittedly, the others are no quicker. One of the soldiers begins to recite something. I hear the word "warrant" and also "suspicion" and "to have murdered."

I look at them one after the other. The other soldiers have positioned themselves behind the one who is speaking. We are sitting at the table. Sidorow's raised hands are trembling from the strain. You shouldn't do that to an old man; I hiss at him that he should lower them but he doesn't listen to me. Jegor shakes his head. Marja is indignant; she stands up slowly, her fists on her hips, the cornflowers fluttering in her hair. And Petrow looks even paler and holds onto Lenotschka.

It is at that moment that I wish I had a cane. I'm not so steady on my legs anymore, and even if I'm younger than Sidorow I should really think long and hard about getting a walker. I stretch out my hand toward his cane. I lift myself up, bracing myself with the cane, and walk over to the soldiers. Then I lift the cane. I just want to get their attention but they step back and point their weapons at me.

"Guests are welcome here, but you must behave like guests." My voice is supposed to thunder, but it just rustles like autumn foliage in the wind. They must have to strain to hear me. "We are celebrating a wedding. And what are you doing?"

The man standing at the front of the soldiers waves a paper. "You are suspected of murder."

"Who is?"

The soldier looks at his documents. Then he tries to look me in the eyes and immediately squints. "All of you."

"All of Tschernowo?"

"I'm sorry, Baba Dunja, but you are not excluded."

And he shows me a line with my name before snatching the paper away again. Apparently he is afraid that his hands will fall off if we both touch the same piece of paper.

"Honored comrade in the service of the military police," I say. "Honored soldier, sir. This can only be some sort of misunderstanding."

Suddenly he waves the paper wildly. "I'm just doing my job, old woman."

"But please look at us, do we look like murderers?"

His gaze wanders over our faces, one after the other. It lingers a little longer on the bridal pair. I decide not to point out their status so he doesn't feel like he's being tricked.

"Don't make this so difficult, Baba Dunja," he forces out between his teeth. "We really have no choice."

My dear granddaughter Laura,

This is your loving grandmother Baba Dunja writing to you from the village of Tschernowo-by-Malyschi. At the moment I'm not actually in Tschernowo but in prison. Please forgive me, then, for the gray paper, I had bought special writing paper with roses on it but I don't have it here.

You are a big girl now and I would like to write to you directly. I find it nice that we are now corresponding. It should be easier for you than for me in one regard because you'll quickly find someone to translate the letter in case you can't understand it. Maybe you can even read Russian but not write it? You young people have it easy when it comes to languages.

I hadn't intended to bother you or your mother with the news. But I heard through the grapevine that it had spread beyond the Russian border. I don't want you to worry unnecessarily. I was told that there are television reports about us. Less on Russian, Ukrainian, and Belarusian stations than on the many foreign ones. Apparently there are a lot of journalists and television crews in front of the prison, and the court can't do its work.

I decided to write you this letter for that reason, so that you hear about things from me and not (only) from your mother or the television. Because the television is a good source of information, but it is also good to hear about the events from someone who was actually there.

I've never been to prison before. It's called pre-trial detention because the crime is not yet proven. But I can't tell you exactly what is different about it from real prison.

Let me describe it.

There are ten women in each cell. The cell isn't very big, more like cozy. Aside from me, Lenotschka and Marja are here, they are two women from Tschernowo. Lenotschka always looks sad because she has no children. She used to worry that they would get sick, so she never had any. I have to say, it was probably a good decision.

Marja is my neighbor. I've already written to you about her. The other women we only met here. Many of them are nice. Tamara had a fight with her husband. Natalja picked up a stranger's baby without asking, Lida mixed up some medications, and Katja insulted a good man, probably by accident.

At first they were worried that we wouldn't be a good fit in the cell together, but the situation has improved.

I haven't seen the men from Tschernowo but I hope they are doing well.

I must confess that your old grandmother has been feeling a bit down here. I sometimes find myself in a bad mood. It's Marja who cheers me up. She makes sure I eat my soup and that I have space on a bottom bunk to sleep, and when we talk she keeps me from getting too melancholy. She says I shouldn't shut down, after all she's the one who just got married and should be far more depressed than me.

Naturally the marriage isn't recognized in prison, and Marja and her newlywed Sidorow are strangers in the eyes of the court and must testify against each other.

My dear granddaughter Laura, I don't know what they are saying on German television. I sometimes glance out the window when I am taken for interrogation. But all I can see is barbed wire and walls.

That's enough for now. I send you a hug, your loving grandmother Baba Dunja.

I know how it feels to be helpless and not to know what to do. But I'm not familiar with the feeling of not knowing what is right and what is wrong. I should have told Laura that I can't read her letter. But I'm a little ashamed about it. And besides, I have to assume that Irina will read my letter, too. I'm not used to thinking about so many angles, I've always been straightforward.

I just hope I haven't disgraced Irina and Laura with this stupid arrest.

It is night in our cell, and I hear the others snoring. It's strange how quickly people get used to one another when they have to. In our cell, I get along particularly well with Tamara, Natalja, Lida, and Katja. Tamara killed her husband with an electric iron. Natalja stole a baby out of a stroller in front of a butcher shop. Lida sold sugar tablets as American aspirin, and Katja spray-painted obscenities on a bishop's garage door.

At first they didn't want to talk to us, they didn't even want to be in the same cell with us because they were afraid of radiation. They banged on the door and screamed until a guard came and switched off the light.

Somewhere in the distance metal utensils clatter. I'm

caged like a guinea pig. We never had a hamster or bird at home, no animal that you had to keep in a cage. I was against locking up animals.

When Marja turns over while she is sleeping the entire cell shakes. I feel very sorry for Marja. Lenotschka less so; she looks no different here than in Tschernowo.

I take out Laura's letter, which I always have with me, and go slowly to the door with it. The light is out in our cell but dull light from the hall comes in through the grated window. I try to read the words but they still make no sense to me, just like so many times before. So I linger on the signature in Latin letters—Laura.

A guard has picked up on the movement in our cell. She walks up to our door with steady, heavy steps. Many of the women here have bodies like men, thick in the middle. The window opens.

"It's me, Baba Dunja," I whisper quickly so she doesn't start shouting and wake up the entire block.

"Go to sleep, granny."

"I can't. Grannies are wakeful."

"Then lie down and button your lips."

"What is your name, daughter?"

She pauses. "Jekaterina."

"That is a beautiful name. Do you know German, Katja?"

She is a big woman. Her face hangs in the window, bloated, round and pale like a full moon. You can tell that she works nights and drinks a lot. And that nobody is waiting for her at home.

"I learned French in school. And if I hear another word out of you, granny, I'm coming in."

I fold Laura's letter until it is small enough to fit into the palm of my hand. My greatest fear is that it will disintegrate before I find out what it says.

My dear granddaughter Laura,

I handed in the first letter, but I doubt you will have received it yet. It is a little difficult for me to write you because I don't know for sure what you are up to. It takes a long time for mail to get from here to you in Germany. My interrogator, the head investigator from the military police, is getting nervous because he's not getting anywhere in clearing up the crime and the dead man's next of kin are getting impatient. I think the dead man must have had a lot of money and people knew his face. What good was it to him?

I now have a lawyer. He is paid by the state and is still quite young. His name is Arkadij Sergejwitsch.

Baba Dunja, he says to me, if all you ever tell me about are the potato bugs in Tschernowo, I can't develop a strategy.

And I say, Strategy? What does an innocent person need a strategy for?

Yesterday he said that a German magazine asked him to put them in touch with me and provided him questions for me. Naturally I wondered whether your mother had something to do with it? Why else would a German magazine be interested in me?

I wanted to tell you a bit more about prison life in general, so I'm not always writing about myself. One can get by here. The girls are getting along with each other better.

Marja saw a report on television that said it was easy to come by drugs in prison but I told her and the others that we weren't having any of that in my cell, that our cell would remain clean. Marja was mad, she said I'd spoil any fun.

And she said the others didn't listen to me because I'm Baba Dunja from Tschernowo. They don't read the papers. They listen to me because they saw the eye tattoo on my hand. In prison, only important people have eye tattoos, and everyone is afraid of them (Marja figured out).

Of course, it's not an eye but a letter O like Oleg. I tried to fill in the O with color because I didn't want it anymore, and that's why it looks strange. Even good ink slowly fades over the course of seventy years. But that's another story.

The food is alright. In the hall by the cafeteria there's a display case where every afternoon they put a sample portion of the soup or gruel so nobody grumbles they got too little. An old woman doesn't need much, I can usually give some of mine to Marja.

I don't want to think about the state of my garden while I'm in here. I hope you are doing well, and that you are getting good grades in school.

Your loving Baba Dunja.

My dear granddaughter Laura,
Baba Dunja writing again. You are probably wondering why I am writing so often now.

It's not just that one has more time in prison. One also has more to write about.

In two days there will be a court hearing. It will take a long time according to Arkadij Sergejewitsch, the little boy with the briefcase. The charges will be read and witnesses will be questioned, and there will be so many of us in the dock, the entire village. There will probably be people in the gallery, too, because the case is so unusual and because some people out there seem to think they know me even though I don't know them. I asked myself whether I should be ashamed and then decided: No, I have no need to be ashamed because I didn't do anything wrong.

I have to think about a few things that I'm going to say in court. I'm not used to speaking in front of a lot of people. But if Arkadij Sergejewitsch reads a statement from me it's possible that some people won't believe the words are really mine. So I have to do it myself.

Whatever you hear about me, never forget: your Baba Dunja holds no one more dear than you, regardless of the fact that we've never seen each other.

During the night I'm awakened by Marja, who is sitting on my cot, crying. I can see the trembling outline of her body. She is trying to be quiet because Tamara, who killed her husband with an electric iron, doesn't like it when anyone makes noise during bedtime hours.

"What is it?" I whisper. Marja just breathes haltingly.

"I don't understand, Maschenka."

I press myself against the wall as she tries to stretch out beside me. It's an awkward undertaking: either Marja is going to crash to the floor or she is going to lie on top of me and suffocate me with her bosom. I suck in my stomach and try to make myself as narrow as possible.

She puts her arm around my neck and presses her lips to my ear.

"I'm so afraid, Dunja," warm tears trickle into my ear canal, "I'm afraid they're going to convict us all and shoot us."

"They're hardly going to shoot us, Marja. Maybe fifty years ago they did that."

"You have it good, nothing ever rattles you."

I don't say anything.

"Obviously it's true that we buried him together, but only one person killed him!"

Marja's tears burn in my ear. I free up a hand and pat her shoulder. She's worse off than I am, her lawyer didn't show up. I asked Arkadij whether he could defend her, too, but he said it was prohibited. I'm getting the impression that a particular chaos prevails here in prison. And then add to that the camera teams outside which disturb everyone as they are working.

"Surely you know who it was, Dunja!" Marja is less and less able to control herself, she is working herself into a hysterical fit. "Please do something so I can go home. I want to go back to Tschernowo. Nobody can bother me there. That's why I moved there, because I thought I'd have peace and quiet, but they found me anyway and locked me up."

My heart begins to palpitate. I press my lips together. She doesn't know that she calls her Alexander's name during the night sometimes.

"Do something! You're the boss!" she sniffles.

"I was never the boss."

But she isn't listening to me. She is trembling and I am trembling with her. "I can't take it anymore, I'm losing my mind in here."

"Calm down," I say. "You have to keep it together, my girl. I'll make sure that you get home. I promise you."

She cries really loudly now, at full volume, until a boot thrown by Tamara silences her.

"Arkadij Sergejewitsch," I say, "how can you find out what language something is?"

"I'm sorry?" he says.

We always meet in the same room. It's square and so small that only a table and two chairs fit in it. The door stays open and now and again a guard sticks a nose in to bark at us or secretly take a photo. Sometimes Arkadij gets up then and goes out and yells. It surprised me that he could be so loud.

He's slight of build, wears a white shirt and a suit, the briefcase sits between us on the table, next to it a portable phone with a big screen that constantly lights up. The dark rings beneath Arkadijs's eyes reach all the way down to his sunken cheeks. He has a wedding ring on his ring finger. Instead of being with his wife, he is squatting here with me, asking me questions that are always the same, leaving me ever less inclined to put in the effort to answer them.

He opens his briefcase and pulls out a bar of chocolate.

The wrapper is printed with golden letters in a foreign script. It's the same alphabet that Laura's letter is written in.

"This is for you," he says.

"Thank you, but it's really not necessary."

"I've been racking my brain trying to think of a way I could make you happy."

"I have everything and am content. Thank you for the kiwi the other day, I hadn't had one in a long time."

"Baba Dunja! I'm at my wit's end."

"What would happen if someone were to confess?" I ask. "Would all the rest be allowed to go home?"

"It would depend."

"On what?"

"On who confessed."

This is the way our talks always go. It's exhausting.

"I'm going back to my cell, Arkadij."

"Wait, please!"

The constant standing up and sitting back down gets to my knees.

"It's impossible to answer your question about finding out what language something is in. There are too many languages on earth," he says.

"And what if it is written on paper?"

He leans back and closes his eyes. For a few seconds he wobbles in his chair like a little boy who is bored in class.

"If the word *the* appears frequently, then it is English. If there is a lot of *der*, *die*, or *das* then it's German. And if you see *un* or *une* then it's French. And with *il* it could be Italian. Or it could also still be French."

I look at him respectfully. "You are so young and already so knowledgeable," I say. "Go home to your wife and get a good night's rest."

Petrow and the other men I see for the first time again on the first day of the court proceedings. We are taken one by one into the holding pen inside the courtroom and sit on a bench inside it. Sidorow's knees are stiff, he remains standing and braces himself on Petrow's shoulder. You didn't have to be a former nurse's assistant to see it: he wasn't going to last long. Though actually I expected everyone to be in worse shape than they are.

I see my Arkadij Sergejewitsch with red spots on his chalk-white face. He is sitting opposite the holding pen. The courtroom is bursting with people, though I expected the room to be bigger. Photographers and camera teams are shuffled past us at short intervals. They call to us but we just stare blankly into their lenses.

We villagers of Tschernowo don't greet each other, we don't even look at each other. It could be construed as impoliteness. But in reality we are all bound to each other and have no need of formalities.

The judge is a sturdy woman with bleached blonde hair. She is wearing a black robe and there's a white bib dangling from the collar. While she speaks I scan the faces in the room. Men and women in suits, in shirts, in jean jackets.

I turn toward Petrow. I have to look at him. I need to ask him my most important question. He stares back at me provocatively. I briefly shake my head. This is the wrong time to act like a defiant child.

I'm going to be dead soon anyway, I read in his eyes. Do you really want me to spend my final days in prison?

I stand up, step up to the lattice of metal bars and knock on it.

The judge pauses in the middle of her oration.

"One needn't drag this out unnecessarily," I say. My rusty old voice clangs through the courtroom.

Arkadij stands up frantically. I motion to him with my hand that he should sit back down.

The judge looks down at me. She has the face of a bank teller from the 1980s. She wears fat rings on her fingers. That comforts me. This woman is from a world I still understand. Perhaps she was one of the first babies I helped deliver. Perhaps I once splinted her leg. Perhaps I pronounced the death of her grandmother. There were so many who passed through during all those years.

"Baba Dunja?" she asks, and everyone laughs. She clears her throat and calls for order. "Pardon me . . . Evdokija Anatoljewna. Are you unwell?"

Evdokija Anatoljewna is the name in my passport. A murmur goes through the room.

"I'm doing fine," I say. "But I need to say something. All of us here in this holding pen are either old or infirm or both. Nobody should be treated this way, it is dishonorable. Please, your majesty . . . unfortunately I don't know your name or your father's name. I don't know the customs here, so I beg your pardon if I do something amiss."

The judge looks at Arkadij. Arkadij looks at me. The uniformed personnel whisper to each other. What follows is a series of gestures and looks. Suddenly I feel weak and try to steady myself on the bars of the pen.

Everyone is looking at me and nobody knows what really happened on that day in Tschernowo. Aside from the dead man, a total of just two people in the world know. I am one of them.

"None of you know what really happened," I say. "Please excuse me for disturbing this proceeding. But in this pen is a one-hundred-year-old man who cannot stand up much longer. I will tell you what this is all about. I'll be brief. We are the last inhabitants of Tschernowo. The dead man, whom this case concerns, wanted to move in as well. He brought his little daughter."

If I thought it was quiet in the court before, then I was wrong. Now it is really quiet.

"Tschernowo is a beautiful place," I say. "A good place for us. We don't chase anyone away. But I would, however, advise against it for someone young and healthy. It's not for everyone. Anyone who takes a little child there in order to exact revenge is an evil person. A child needs a mother and clean air."

I fix my gaze on the judge's white bib. I have to concentrate. For a second the thought crosses my mind that she probably doesn't speak English either.

"And now I ask that you take note of the following statement. Arkadij, let me be, I am an old woman and sound of mind. Listen, your majesty. I, Baba Dunja of Tschernowo, killed the evil man with an axe and forced the others under threat of violence to help me dig a grave for him in the garden. It was impossible for them to resist me. I wish to hereby petition your grace to release the others and punish me as the sole perpetrator."

My dear granddaughter Laura,

I hope you and your mother and, naturally, your father, whom I hold in high esteem, are doing well.

I am using my fifteen-minute break from work to write you, as long as there is still light. You must have

seen on television that your grandmother is now a felon.
I was sentenced to three years' imprisonment for volun-
tary manslaughter.

I'm a little bit ashamed to write you, because you are
probably ashamed of me. But you needn't be. First,
because my conscience is clear. I only did what needed to
be done. Second, because you would be a good girl even
if you did have a crazy person for a grandmother.

I keep your photo with me, the one where you are
wearing a red T-shirt. I don't have many things here, just
a few things for daily use. I often think about my beautiful house in Tschernowo. It looks now as if I won't die
there after all, as I wanted. I haven't gotten used to this
thought yet. Believe me, Laura, I have experienced a lot
in my life. But my most peaceful years I spent there.

Now I am housed in a camp. But life is fine here. I get
along with the other girls. We are awoken at six, and
after washing up and eating breakfast (barley mush), we
go to the sewing machines in the workshops. We sew pillowcases. I am permitted to receive six packages per year
but I made sure not to write that to your mother because
I don't want her to start unnecessarily spending money
on me again.

In addition, we are allowed four multiday visits and
six short visits of up to three hours each. It's a shame that
you are so far away and can't visit me. It's also too far for
Marja. Arkadij signs up for short visits as if he has nothing else to do. We are separated by a glass partition and
speak by way of a telephone handset. He can't say anything mean about anyone though, because if he does the
guard who listens in on all conversations will interrupt us
immediately. So he reads to me from the magazine

Gardening Today. *Once we had trouble because the warden mistook a manure schedule for a coded message.*

I don't count the days any more than I did in Tschernowo or anywhere else.

I don't manage to finish this letter. My hand refuses to cooperate any longer. I try to stretch my fingers but they remain cramped. I look distrustfully on my treasonous appendages, which have never before left me in the lurch, and extricate the pen with the help of the other hand. Then I want to stand up. I realize just in time that I'm not able to, and I remain seated. A fall with a possible broken hip as a consequence is not something I need.

I sit there for what must be half an hour. Maybe more and maybe less. Then I try to call for help, but I'm not able. Slowly my eyes start to close. I know exactly what is happening to me, but the word for it escapes me. My back hurts from sitting too long. When will they come looking for me, I should have been back at work ages ago. Someone turns me onto my back—I hadn't even noticed that I'd fallen over.

Some say the soul can leave the body and hover above it and decide up there whether to return to this shell. I don't know if there's anything to it, for I was raised a materialist. We didn't go in for souls and baptism and paradise and hell. I also don't hover over my bed, I lie in it. Out of one eye I look at Irina. Out of the other, Arkadij. I try to merge the two eyes. Against the wall I recognize an IV stand.

I'm wearing an unfamiliar nightgown and the covers are pulled up to my stomach. The only time I've been to the hospital in my entire life was for the birth of my children. I got pregnant with Alexej before Irina was even one year old. I had thought that nursing prevented pregnancy, and since I had waited so long for Irina I didn't expect to have a second child at all.

Jegor was angry at me. During my second pregnancy he was rarely at home, and he made no attempt to explain away the absences as work trips. When he showed up back at home he smelled of cheap perfume. I've hated perfume ever since. I hadn't planned to let Jegor back into the house at all. But then my water broke a few weeks early and somebody had to stay with little Irina while I gave birth to her brother. The fact that it was a boy filled Jegor with pride; the fact that it was a premature birth, with feelings of guilt. Jegor kissed my hands and cried in my lap.

I open my eyes again.

This is the second time in my life that I've seen Irina crying. She is sitting on a plastic chair beside my bed, a stack of photocopies in her hands.

I don't understand the reason for her tears, since I'm doing well, after all, and I want to get out of here. I certainly must have missed time at my sewing machine. I didn't come to prison to end up lying in bed.

I tell Irina exactly that.

"Do you want to look in the mirror, Mother?" Irina asks. I can feel that the corner of my mouth is sagging. But that never stopped anyone from sewing straight seams. And anyway, she is the last person who should be criticizing my outward appearance. Since the last time I've seen her she has aged decades.

"You didn't need to come," I say. "You'll be in trouble at work."

Irina startles me with the news that she has already been in the country for more than two weeks. She must have taken unpaid leave, German doctors couldn't possibly take so much time off. Don't want her to lose her job on top of it. Instead of cutting open German soldiers and stitching them up again, she has flown here. I learn that she has spent days together with my lawyer fighting for me to be transferred to a decent hospital. Even now her phone rings, and she says Amnesty is on the line. But I've never heard of that woman.

"And nobody is watering my tomatoes in Tschernowo," I think out loud.

"Forget the tomatoes, Mother. In Germany we will lease a garden plot for you."

"What is there for me in Germany? I don't know anyone there except you."

"But everyone knows you," says Irina, holding up a photocopy of a magazine.

Seeing the photo frightens me. I wasn't even photographed much as a young girl, and with good reason. The fact that I'm on the cover of a German magazine with my headscarf, my wrinkles, and my still fairly good teeth is proof that the outside world has gone crazy.

I look at more photos. Photos of Tschernowo in black and white. I remember the photographer who spoke a language we didn't understand. He had a high-strung interpreter with him and took pictures of everything, Marja and her goat, Lenotschka and her apple trees, Sidorow and his telephone.

These are the photos that came out of that.

Even Konstantin is captured here. And I am standing in front of my house with the cats skulking at my feet.

There is a lot of writing. The photos are old, but the magazine is new. She copied the pages out of the latest issue. Irina reads the piece to me, a bit haltingly since she has to translate it as she goes.

"Baba Dunja is one of those women you envy because they can smile like children. She has a small, wrinkled face and narrow, dark-brown eyes. She is tiny and as round as a ball—she's not even five feet tall. An iconic figure. An invention of the international press. A modern myth."

I look at my hands. On the back of one, the faded O between the liver spots, which really does look a little like an eye. I didn't want to live when Oleg took up with another girl, and now I can't even picture his face any-more.

"I'm not an invention. I actually exist, right, Irina?"

And once again Irina starts to cry like a small child.

I would like peace to return. I would like to go back to work. Right now I'm still too weak on my feet, but I'll get there. I would like to dress myself like a human being. I would like Irina to go home. And I would like to find out what is distressing her so much. She doesn't want to tell me. She wants to talk about what is in the papers, what the world thinks of me, but what do I care about the world?

"Did Laura read my letters?"

"Laura?" Something in her face scares me.

"Yes. Laura. Did the letters arrive?"

"We haven't received any letters from you in ages, Mother."

"But I wrote to her."

"Maybe you didn't put on the right postage."

"But I explained everything in them."

She shrugs her shoulders. She doesn't need my explanation. Nobody needs explanations. People need peace and perhaps a little money.

"How is Laura?" I ask.

"Laura?" she repeats again. And the way she says it sends a shiver down my spine. Because I realize I am about to learn something terrible.

"Laura is ill?" My lips go numb with anxiety.

Irina shakes her head. And then I think I should have known. Should have figured it out long ago, because all the signs point to it. "There is no Laura, right? You made her up. You are unable to have children. Or you don't want to. Like Lenotschka."

Irina looks at me. Her eyes are open wide and very blue. If she didn't have such a severe face she would be beautiful. But I didn't bring her up to be a beautiful woman. I tried to get her through it. That at least I managed.

And in my head is just one thought: What is the point of it all if Laura doesn't exist?

"Of course she exists," says Irina. "But she is very different than you think."

The Laura I know is blonde and has sad eyes. Her face is so pretty it almost hurts. She doesn't wear hair clips and never smiles. She is a marvel because she's perfect. That's the way my Laura is in the photos.

The Laura Irina speaks about has shaved her head. She has stolen money from her parents, had alcohol poisoning at age thirteen, has been thrown out of two schools, and doesn't understand much Russian, which I don't hold against her.

"She hates me," says Irina and looks right through me with her rubbed-red eyes.

Irina has never spoken with me like this. She has never mentioned any problems. And now one like this, all at once. She needs to be hugged but we're not accustomed to that.

"I've done everything wrong, Mother."

"No," I say. "I have done everything wrong. It breaks my heart that you have so many problems, and then I add to them with my murder. I just hope your husband doesn't think badly about our family."

"No idea what he thinks. We've been divorced for seven years."

She says this casually, and I nod just as casually. What can you do. Children are more important. Our child is in trouble. And given that revelation, everything else pales by comparison—the conviction, my stroke, and the pillowcases in the prison.

"I can't even give you the money I've been saving for Laura. It's in a tea caddy in Tschernowo. Maybe someone can go get it."

"I couldn't give it to her anyway. I don't know where she is."

"I don't understand."

"What is there to understand? Laura ran away. She has been missing for months. She doesn't check in with me. I have no idea where she is."

And for that reason I say something that I am sure will help Irina. "Laura wrote me a letter."

Once again I can't say whether what I'm doing is right or wrong. I ask Irina to give me my plastic bag, which someone has placed next to the bed. I unpack: a bar of soap in a soapbox, a sponge, a half-empty tube of hand cream, and another of toothpaste. The red lipstick that Marja lent me for my time in prison. And the small, folded-up piece of paper that I open and smooth out.

"All I could understand was *the*," I say. "I wasn't able to find anyone who could translate it for me."

Irina rips the letter from my hands a little too hastily. My betrayal of Laura's trust pains my soul. But Irina needs this now. She bends over the sheet of paper, her lips move silently.

"What does it say? Can you read it?"

She doesn't answer, her eyes jump around the page, and her chin begins to tremble.

"Tell me, Irina."

She lifts her head and looks at me. "It says exactly what I told you. What a screwed-up life she's led. How awful her family is."

"I'm sure she doesn't mean it."

"Oh, yes, she does. It says she hates us all. Just not you."

"And where is she now?"

"Unfortunately, it doesn't say."

I know that Irina lied. There was more in the letter than she told me. She left quickly and said that she would come back as soon as possible. I told her not to worry about me. I will be just fine. She needs to tend to her child. I don't want to believe all the stories she told about Laura. Laura is a good girl.

"You are still young and can even marry again if you would just learn to smile and to buy yourself some nice clothes," I told her as she was leaving.

"From whom would I have learned how to do that?"

"I eventually learned it, too. And I was over seventy by then. I really only learned to smile after I moved back to Tschernowo."

She cringed.

I took back the letter and this time hid it in a shoe. Irina didn't like it, but I stood firm. She was allowed to read the letter but it belongs to me. And now I know it is written in English. Good girl, she probably thought her grandmother could speak a foreign language. Or that it would be easier for me to find someone to translate English than German.

I have my spot at the sewing machine back. As long as I have work to do, I can breathe easily. Our country needs pillowcases.

I've stopped writing letters. I'm trying to learn English instead. I got lucky: the woman who sits at the machine to my left can still remember her English lessons from school. She's twenty-one years old and is serving a sentence for something she did to her newborn child. She doesn't talk about it and I don't ask. She teaches me an English word every day; in exchange I help her with her sewing.

My fingers feel as if they no longer belong to me. I pay no attention. Since the stroke I've sewn six hundred and fourteen pillowcases. That's not so many, younger women work twice or even three times as fast as I do. But six hundred and fourteen people no longer have to sleep on bare pillows thanks to me.

At noon, as always, we have a break, we get ourselves thin fruit tea from the canister, most of the women go out into the yard for a smoke, I stand up and do some vein exercises and watch the sparrows as they flit between all the feet in rubber shoes looking for invisible crumbs. I think of the bullfinches of Tschernowo and wonder if I'll ever come face-to-face with a crane again. In between I repeat the English words I've learned in the last few days. *Bag. Eat. Teacher. Girl.*

I'm not finished with pillowcase number six hundred and fifteen when a commotion erupts outside. I don't look up; I'll learn soon enough what it's about. When they come inside I'm startled because they make a beeline for me. This can't be good, I think, when so many come to get me. It is women in uniform and men in civilian clothes and vice versa, their faces blur together, and I feel very old.

One of them steps forward, stoops down to me, and says loudly that our president has pardoned me.

Our president is a good man. He looks a little like Jegor in his good years. Except that Jegor was a dishrag and our president is a man of iron will. With a man like him I would have had more respect for my marriage. He wouldn't have shown any fear of Tschernowo, he wouldn't have let himself be forced to abandon his village, he would have laughed at the offer of compensation and at the pointless vision tests and the vitamins that you received for free as a reactor victim.

Because our constitution is celebrating an anniversary, the president has pardoned a lot of criminals. I'm one of them. My crime is more serious than many others, but my age must have swayed him. Maybe he read about me in the paper and thought, Baba Dunja from Tschernowo should not die in prison. He has a soft heart, like all great men.

I'm just sorry about the pillowcase I've started. I make every one like it's my last, and this one isn't finished, and it bothers me. I'm urged to hurry along because I'm now free. I'm not prepared for this. I don't know what to do. Pack up your things, they say. So I pack.

I don't have much, the clothes belong to the prison, I lay them out tidily. Someone keeps looking into the cell. I hiss at him, hasn't he ever seen an old woman fold three pairs of underpants. I make the bed and fluff the pillow. My things I place in the pillowcase, which I then tie closed.

I'm not surprised to see Arkadij. He probably wants to make sure everything is done properly and that nobody swaps my blood thinning medication for toilet cleaning fluid, as happened recently.

Arkadij urges me to hurry. So that I can leave in peace, the press has been told that I won't be released for another three days. But soon the first of them will arrive, as rumors travel fast. He braces me, I have to make an effort to keep up with him step for step. We cross the yard, I want to go to the workshop one last time to say my goodbyes. Arkadij holds me back as if his only concern is to get out of here as quickly as possible. The young woman who sits next to me runs up and shoves a rolled-up piece of paper into my hand.

"English vocabulary," she whispers. I run my hand

across her delicate cheek and wish her many more healthy children. Then I turn toward the workshop. Women in gray prison clothes are standing at the window. And then they applaud.

Arkadij Sergejewitsch drives a dirty little car. He has brought me a new, slightly too long winter jacket and gloves because I had to hand in my warm clothes to the prison. I feel bad that criminals like me keep him from making decent money. He didn't get a single ruble from me for his work. I'll have to give him some money from Laura's tea caddy.

"As soon as I get home I'm going to send you money."

"Better just to hurry, Baba Dunja," he says and holds open the car door for me. And so in my old age I take a ride in a private car.

Arkadij says we can get everything I need at the airport.

"Get what? At what airport?"

"You are flying to your daughter's in Germany. It is all arranged."

"I am not flying anywhere," I say. "I am going home."

Arkadij understands immediately.

The little television on his dashboard that tells him where to go doesn't recognize Tschernowo.

"My garden is surely overgrown," I say. "Maybe you can drop me at the bus station."

"Your daughter would kill me," says Arkadij.

He stops briefly in Malyschi to buy a chocolate bar and a bottle of water. Never before has a strange man spent money on food for me.

"You are a good boy," I say, sticking the things in my pocket.

He just looks at me. It's the same later during the drive. It would be a shame if I were to die in a car crash now, of all times, and just because he didn't keep his eyes on the road.

I ask him about his life and work. We'd never had the chance to talk about anything but the axe in the head. He answers cautiously, as if every word were a step in a mine-field. Then he says he's going to become a father in two months.

"Congratulations from the bottom of my heart!" I say. "The child is surely healthy? These days you can see right inside."

"My wife isn't here," he says. "I sent her to England."

I nod. Then I tell him about the flowers in my garden as he drives along a country road. The landscape stretches out cheerfully white before me. The winters keep getting milder. When I was little we had more snow. Nature needs the snow in order to rest.

In Arkadij's car, you sit much lower to the ground than in a bus and you hear the pebbles stirred up by the tires. The drive goes by quickly. He stops in front of the aban-doned candy factory, next to the green shelter of the bus stop, which is dusted with snow. This is where I always recuperated after my long marches. On the path through the fields you can see the prints of rabbit paws.

"I'm sorry, Baba Dunja," says Arkadij, avoiding my gaze.

"Don't let it trouble you," I say. "I'm very grateful to you."

"I just don't know what to say."

"Then don't say anything."

I have to struggle to get out. He opens the door for me

and waits patiently. He hands me the pillowcase with my
things in it.

"You still know the way?"

"You bet I do." I brush a few snowflakes from his
sleeve. "Thank you for your dedication."

Then he is gone. I throw the half-full pillowcase over
my shoulder and head on my way.

I walk not one hour or two. I walk more than three
hours. It's as if the way has lengthened, as if Tschernowo
has receded during the time I wasn't there. Something is
singing inside me even though I am having trouble breathing. I limp since the stroke, and everything hurts when I
walk as a result. I keep stopping to catch my breath. I wonder whether I should just leave the pillowcase behind.

On the other hand: Who would leave their underwear
in a field except in an emergency?

I sing "The Apple and Pear Trees Are Blooming" to
regain my strength.

Fortunately it's not summer. The heat would kill me.

Soon spring will come to Tschernowo. Fresh grass will
sprout, the trees will subtly start to green. I will go into the
woods and tap birch sap. Not because I want to live to be
a hundred but because it is a crime to reject the gifts of
nature. The birds will twitter in the blossoming apple
trees. The biologist told me why the birds are louder here
than elsewhere. After the reactor, more males survived
than females. This imbalance persists to this day. And it is
the desperate males who belt out their songs in search of
good females.

I wonder whether I will still run across Petrow.
Probably not. I wouldn't bet that Sidorow is still around,
either. Maybe they will greet me as ghosts. My cat is surely

still there. And Mrs. Gavrilow's chickens. The house will certainly need to be made inhabitable again. Jegor will be there. He will always be there.

I catch my breath again. My leg hurts, but I must keep going. The houses of Tschernowo rise on the horizon like a set of loose, crooked teeth.

Hopefully nobody is there, I think. If nobody is there, then I will live alone with all the ghosts and animals. And wait to see who all comes along.

I think of Laura. I will always think of Laura. I think about how nice it would have been if we had overtaken the bus on the drive here, and inside the bus had been a blonde girl. A short-haired, tattooed blonde girl for all I care. She would have hopped out and I would have taken her by the hand and taken her home. That is what has always been missing for this girl. She never had a home because I never taught her mother how to feel comfortable in life. I learned it too late myself.

I will study English and read Laura's letter. I will stay alive until I can read her letter.

I take the chocolate bar out of the pillowcase to strengthen myself.

The main road is covered in fresh snow. Smoke rises from the Gavrilows' chimney. And Marja's goat is nibbling on the bark of my apple tree.

"Pssst," I call. "Get away from there, you stupid animal!"

The goat jumps to the side. Marja appears in her window.

"Who's yelling at my goat?" she shouts.

I have the feeling that I'm seeing double. Just a second ago she was in the window and now she is storming out the door. She runs up to me and nearly crushes me in her embrace.

"Let go of me," I scold. "You're going to break all my bones. I'm not eighty-two anymore."

"I knew they would release you," she whispers. "I knew it all along."

"How? I didn't know."

"You have to come to my place, the spiders have taken over yours."

"First I have to have a look." I turn my back to Marja and my face to my house. It is still my house, the spiders will understand.

"Eat something first!"

"Later," I say. I walk over and put my hand on the door handle. A meow wafts out of the shed and a little kitty, gray like smoke, straggles out.

"Your cat had another litter," shouts Marja. "One of them is missing an eye."

"Don't yell like that," I say. "You're not alone anymore."

And then I push open the door and once again I am home.

ABOUT THE AUTHOR

Russian-born Alina Bronsky is the author of *Broken Glass Park* (Europa, 2010); *The Hottest Dishes of the Tartar Cuisine* (Europa, 2011), named a Best Book of 2011 by *The Wall Street Journal*, *The Huffington Post*, and *Publishers Weekly*; and *Just Call Me Superhero* (Europa, 2014).